ISBN: 979-8-9859829-5-4

Book/Cover Design by: **MATT DURAND**

A DECLAN WYLER NOVEL

TRACK DOGS

MATT DURAND

Chapter 1

The beat up white Chevy Silverado coasted along a deserted road toward what Clayton Judge hoped was his salvation. He squinted into the distance, scanning the tree line to his right for a break in the foliage. A blanket of fog cut his visibility to ten feet. Annoyed, Clayton twisted the dial of the headlights to their lowest setting, reducing the glare. He brushed away the sweat dripping down his thick neck and wiped the moisture from his hand on the worn fabric of the seat. Without looking, his fingers jostled the A/C knob. When it refused to turn farther, he cursed under his breath and rolled down his window, letting in the humid night air.

"Where the fuck's this road?" Clayton said.

His cousin Jed consulted a handheld GPS.

"Should be right here," he said, glancing up from the screen, and peering into the darkness.

"Well, I don't see shit, do you?"

"Not yet."

"If we're late…"

"Relax. We'll find it. The map shows we're right on top of it. Slow down."

"I go any slower, we won't be moving," Clayton said. "This fucking fog."

"What's that?"

"What?"

"That. Right there," Jed said, pointing a crooked finger into the windshield.

Clayton slowed the truck to a crawl, searching the area where his cousin's finger directed him. A small red reflector nailed to a tree flickered ten yards away as the headlights swept past. When they came even with the spot, Clayton noticed a dirt path barely wide enough for the truck to fit into.

"Turn here," Jed said.

Before Clayton turned the wheel, his eyes darted to the rearview mirror for any signs of life. He didn't know who he expected to see behind him at eleven at night in the middle of nowhere, but since recent events in his life put him into a situation he didn't want to be in, he found himself checking over his shoulder more and more.

"What are you waiting for?" Jed said.

"Nothing," Clayton said. He stared in the mirror a moment longer, then returned his gaze to the path. Clayton thought he wouldn't be here now if it weren't for his father. Instead, he could've been at Darlenes, having her work that magic tongue over his package while he sipped some rum-drenched sweet tea. Clayton spit out the window, imagining the wad landing on his father's grave.

The truck bumped over the ground and disappeared into the woods.

"Christ, you think the trailer will hold?" Jed said, grabbing the handle above the window and looking out the back.

"It'll hold."

Clayton white-knuckled the steering wheel, slowly maneuvering along the winding path.

"How long are we on this for?" Clayton said, keeping his eyes forward.

"About another mile, it looks like."

Another mile, and then the real test would come. If his plan didn't work, his life wouldn't be worth much. Enzo would either put a bullet between his eyes or make his life so miserable he'd kill himself. He could run, which he'd considered his best option for a while, but if he thought he was paranoid now, a life of being constantly chased would be unbearable. The two men rode on in silence until the path leveled out, then opened into a clearing about the size of half of a basketball court.

"This is the spot," Jed said. He held the device out for Clayton to see. A white circle pulsed on the screen representing their current location. The dot rested on top of a marker pin. Clayton nodded in confirmation, then drove along the edge a little way before angling the truck toward the path they'd emerged from. He reversed, putting the trailer five feet from the opening on the opposite side of the tree line. Clayton flipped the truck lights off and killed the engine. He didn't move, letting his ears adjust to the sounds of nature until they replaced the dull rumble of the diesel engine. Jed pulled a beer from his backpack at his feet and cracked the can open.

"What the hell are you doing?" Clayton said. "Put that shit away until we're done here."

Jed looked at his cousin as if he'd slapped him. "It's just a beer.

These woods creep me the hell out. I need something to take the edge off. Steady my nerves."

Clayton shot his arm out and snatched the beer from Jed's hand. Part of the contents sloshed onto Jed's shirt.

"Jesus, Clayton. I just washed this fucking shirt."

Clayton poured the beer out the window. When he emptied it, he crushed the can and tossed it at Jed's face, hitting him in the side of the head.

"Don't be fucking stupid," Clayton said. "You're in this thing now. Don't forget who owes who. If it wasn't for me you'd be doing life or waiting for a fucking lethal injection. So you do what you're told. We screw this up, and our lives don't mean shit."

"You're right," Jed said, frowning while massaging his temple. "You're right. I owe you big. I'm here, though, aren't I?"

"Yeah, you're here physically, but what about mentally? I need to know I can count on you to see this thing through to the end no matter what."

"Yeah, man. I'm good," Jed said. "Shit, sorry. It was a beer. I didn't see the harm."

"I know you didn't, and that's the problem."

"Ah, come on, Clayton, lighten up."

Clayton considered a further tongue-lashing, but he knew Jed had a sensitive streak in him. If Clayton pushed him too far, Jed would recede into himself and become a problem instead of a helping hand.

"Radio those guys and tell them we're here," Clayton said.

Jed grumbled as he rifled through his backpack until he found the walkie-talkie given to him by the Alabama crew. He twisted the knob, powering on the old-school communication device.

"Bama Boys, this is the Croc Cousins. We're in position. Do

you copy?" Jed grinned at Clayton as he released the walkie button. Silence filled the cab. To Clayton, each passing second made his mind think the worse. *Had they missed the drop time? Did the Bama Boys leave already? Did they back out of the arrangement? What then? Would Enzo give him any more chances to make things right?* A twig snapped in the distance. Clayton whipped his head toward the sound. *Or had Enzo never intended to give him a chance? Were there guns trained on them right now? Were they waiting for them to get out of the truck before they blew their heads off?*

"Try them again," Clayton said as he nervously scanned the slumbering trees for any discernible human forms.

"Bama Boys, we are in position. Do you copy?"

More silence.

"Where the fuck are these guys?" Clayton said.

"Do you think they bailed?"

"How the hell would I know that?"

"Man, I hate these woods."

Another snapping sound caught Clayton's attention. "Did you hear that?

Jed rolled down his window and listened.

"No, I don't hear nothing."

Static erupted out of the walkie-talkie then, and both men jumped at the sudden noise. A low gravelly voice came through.

"This is the Bama Boys," the voice said. "We copy, Croc Cousins. Over."

Clayton closed his eyes and released a long sigh. He wiped the sweat forming on his forehead with the back of his hand.

"Are you ready for us?" Jed said into the walkie.

"Yeah, we been ready," the voice responded.

"Ok, we're prepping them now. Hang tight. Over."

Clayton removed the keys, then grabbed a flashlight from a cupholder. "Let's get a move on," he said, opening his door. As his feet touched the earth, Clayton clicked on the flashlight and hesitated behind the door. He panned the beam into the woods, where he thought he'd heard the noises. Nothing moved. *Keep it together. You're imagining things.*

At the back of the trailer, Clayton unlocked the door and swung it open. The stench of shit, dirty animals, and gasoline assaulted him. He staggered from the door. It took all of his concentration to avoid puking. After spitting the taste from his mouth and blowing a snot rocket from his nose, he stripped off his sweaty t-shirt and tied it around his face. The scent of the shirt wasn't much better, but it beat the reeking odors of the trailer. Jed climbed into the putrid space, apparently oblivious to the noxious smells. A few yips and whimpers came from inside as Jed untethered the ATV and then wheeled it to the entrance. Clayton helped him lower it to the ground. Jed grabbed a duffle bag and hopped out of the trailer. From the bag, he extracted a large controller with a makeshift screen attached to the top. He fired up the ATV and switched on the camera mounted to the front. After a few seconds, the screen displayed a live feed from the camera. Using the controller, Jed manipulated the pistons and pulleys attached to the ATV he custom made to remotely propel it forward. As the driverless vehicle headed toward the mouth of the second path, Clayton said, "Son of a bitch. I can't believe that thing works."

"I told you I could do it," Jed said.

Once Jed stopped the ATV at the second entrance, he set down the controller and reached into the bag. He handed two battery-powered lights to Clayton and kept two for himself. The men grunted and cursed as they affixed the lights to a support beam of their own design across the rear of the vehicle.

"You can handle the rabbit?" Clayton said.

"Yeah, I got it."

Clayton returned to the trailer, lifting the flap of his makeshift mask for a last breath of fresh air before entering. He shone the light into the four cages, revealing the standing bodies of the greyhounds. Clayton never got used to the sight of the dogs, despite being around them as far back as he could remember. Their slender frames and odd proportions gave them an alien quality he found unsettling. As a kid, he disliked dogs in general, but he especially disliked these greyhounds, as they stole his father's attention from him. After his father's death, though, his resentment turned into a burning hatred when the ugly mutts got forced onto him. Every bad break he'd received in his life, he tied to the dogs, whether it was justified or not. If he had his way, he would've thrown all of the freak breed into a pool of gasoline and watched them burn. The plan he hatched now, Clayton reminded himself, exacted some shred of revenge.

Clayton kicked the cages and shouted. "Come on, you ugly bastards. On your feet. Time to earn your keep."

When the dogs rose, Clayton opened the first cage and dragged the dog out by the scruff of his neck. He attached a foot-long rope to the collar, then pulled the dog to the next cage, repeating the process until he held two leashes in each hand. Clayton led the four dogs out of the trailer and walked them to Jed.

"Did you finish up?" Clayton said.

"Yeah. Ready to go."

"Give them the shots first. Don't need any of these fuckers

crapping out before they get to the other side."

Jed pulled a book-sized pouch from the duffle bag. From the pouch, he extracted four prefilled hypodermic needles. He yanked off the cap of the first needle with his teeth.

"Hold them still," Jed said.

Clayton retracted the leashes so the dogs were smushed together against his legs. Jed walked behind the dogs and jabbed a needle into the hindquarters of each.

"All set," Jed said. "Nothing like a shot of nose candy to give them a little giddy-up and go." He laughed as he tossed the spent needles into the pouch.

"Tell them we're ready," Clayton said.

Jed pressed the button on the walkie. "We're locked and loaded. Ready on your word. Over."

The walkie crackled. "Make it snappy. Over."

Jed clipped the walkie to his belt. "It's showtime, Cuz."

"Don't stop for anything."

Jed nodded, then picked up the controller. He hit the lights switch on the ATV's back. The dogs yipped and bucked at the sight of the fake rabbit. He revved the engine a few times before giving Clayton a final thumbs-up. Clayton forced the dogs behind the ATV, five feet back. The modified vehicle leaped forward, releasing a cloud of dirty smoke. The lights bounced over the path. When Jed put twenty feet between them, Clayton dropped the leashes. The dogs sprinted after the fleeing quad and zeroed in on the taunting rabbit. Clayton despised the greyhounds, but their speed never ceased to amaze him. His father told him once some greyhounds ran as fast as 45 mph. Jed's ATV had just enough juice to keep ahead of the dogs. From what Clayton and Jed timed out, the trip to the collection point should take under two minutes.

Clayton followed the fading lights until a slight depression in the terrain blocked his view. He removed the t-shirt from his face and pulled it over his sticky skin. With the flashlight, he checked his watch, calculating an approximate arrival time. The waiting was the worst part. He hovered over Jed's shoulder, studying the screen as the ATV sped over the terrain.

"Keep that thing straight," Clayton said.

"I've got this."

"Don't swerve so much."

"Get out of here, would you?" Jed said, raising his voice. "I know what the fuck I'm doing. You're making me nervous watching over my goddamn shoulder. Go do something."

"Like what?"

"Go jerk off for all I care."

Clayton stomped over to the truck. He grabbed a pack of cigarettes from the glove compartment and lit one. The rush of nicotine steadied his nerves. He rechecked his watch. The ATV should get to the drop point soon. The Bama Boys would take the dogs, Jed would bring back the ATV, and they'd be on their way. *Might even have enough time to roust Darlene for a quickie.* He smiled, picturing her ample tits slapping against his face. While Clayton smoked, he paced alongside the trailer. Ten minutes later, he finished the cigarette and flicked the butt away. Something felt off to him. Things were taking too long. He returned to Jed's side.

"Did they get there?" Clayton said, peering at the screen.

"Yeah, I parked it."

"And?"

"And what? They haven't said anything yet."

"What the fuck's going on?"

Clayton considered radioing over to the Bama Bros, but he

didn't want to come across as nervous. With men like them, any sign of weakness would be exploited. He'd give them another few minutes to respond, then make contact.

Clayton lit another cigarette, grabbed the walkie, then walked to the path entrance. He strained his eyes into the black horizon, hoping to pick out a flourish of light.

"Come on, already," Clayton mumbled between puffs on his cigarette. Then Jed's walkie-talkie buzzed. Clayton hustled to his side.

"This is Bama Boys, over."

"Answer it," Clayton said.

"We all set?" Jed said.

"There's a problem," the Bama Boy said.

Clayton and Jed stared at each other.

"What kind of problem?" Jed said.

"One of the dogs is missing?"

"You don't have four?"

"Only got three here."

"Well, we sent all four."

"You sure about that? Not trying to hold out on us, are you?"

"Fuck no. We sent four."

"We've only got three."

"Maybe it's just slower. Give it a few minutes."

"We've already given it a few minutes."

Clayton crumpled the cigarette between his fingers. *This isn't happening.* He snatched the walkie-talkie from Jed's hand.

"We sent four. Check the woods."

No response came for a few seconds. Then the Bama Boy said, "We're not checking shit. This is on you."

Jed stared at Clayton. "Should we go look for it?"

He hesitated, thinking. "We're going to have to at least try."

"We'll see what we can find," Clayton said into the walkie-talkie. "Give us some time."

"You've got ten minutes."

"Ten minutes?" Jed said, rubbing his knuckles. "There's miles of woods out there. What are we going to find in ten minutes?

"Fuck me," Clayton said. "Grab your light, and let's fucking move."

They jogged down the path, each man dedicating their light to one side of the treeline. When they got to the halfway point, tired and out of breath and with no sign of the dog, Clayton stopped.

"This is fucking crazy," he said. "We're not going to find that bitch."

"So what are we going to do?"

"Give me the damn mic."

Jed tossed the walkie-talkie to Clayton. He steadied his breathing and then spoke.

"Bama Boys," he said. "We checked as far as we could go. There's no sign of the dog. But it's as good as dead, anyway. Between the shitty shape of the bitch, the lack of people, and all the predators living in these woods, how far will the dog get? Not far. The plan is still intact. Even if someone finds the dog, nothing ties it to any of us. We'll make sure an extra dog is in the next run too. Ok?"

A long silence hung heavy in the night air like a guillotine ready to fall. Clayton spoke into the device again.

"Do you copy?"

Some static registered, and then the Bama Boy said, "We copy. But we're going to have to relay this information to our boss. You understand that, right?"

It meant word would get back to Enzo. This part of the equation worried Clayton the most. *Would Enzo see losing one of the dogs as a part of doing business? Breakage. Isn't that what people called it? Or would he consider their maiden voyage a failure and shut down the whole operation and possibly Clayton along with it?* Only time would tell, he figured. What other choices did he have?

"I understand."

"Alright, we're leaving now, then."

Clayton tossed the walkie-talkie back to Jed. "Bring the ATV back, and let's get the fuck out of here."

"What do you think Enzo is going to say?"

Ignoring the question, Clayton shook his head as he headed back to the truck. He had an idea about what Enzo would say, or rather what he would do, and the thought of it made him sick to his stomach.

Chapter 2

With the flick of the dealer's wrist, the cards spun across the felt table. When the second card skidded to a stop in front of Declan Wyler, he didn't immediately pick the pair up. Instead, as he'd done for the last four hours of the tournament, he studied the five other players at the table as they sized up the strength of their cards. Of the six seats, Wyler occupied the third chair. He knew three of the players. In the first chair sat Barry, a high roller who worked in Big Tech. As his eyes passed over his cards, Barry pinched the inside of his lip with his teeth. It took Wyler about three months to notice the tell, but the movement generally signaled a hand Barry would try bluffing, an artform he'd yet to master. One of the two newcomers sat in the second seat. A short well dressed black guy that played sharp but, at times, too conservatively. He introduced himself as Cedrick. The fourth and fifth seats held a set of fraternal twins, Greg and Mallory. Both were decent players, but Wyler found them slightly weaker when they played the same table.

In the sixth seat sat the other newcomer. She told the group her name was Josephine, but something about how she said it led Wyler to believe it wasn't her real name. The way the word rolled off her tongue lacked a degree of naturalness that comes with saying the same name since childhood. She had beautiful features Wyler guessed were Middle Eastern in origin. When she spoke, Wyler didn't detect any discernible accent. Her casual attire of skinny jeans and stylish t-shirt sought to blend in, but it couldn't quite cover hints she came from wealth. Despite his best efforts, Wyler couldn't decipher any clear tells. As a result, most of the night, she controlled the table.

Wyler observed every inch of her as she glanced at her cards. Then he caught something. Josephine ran her thumb across a ring on her index finger. The motion was subtle and lasted all but a second. Wyler replayed the hands from the night's start. Had he seen her make that movement before? He felt she had, but he couldn't be sure. *What hand had it happened on? Had she won the pot then? Or did she bluff the hand?* The memories lacked the sharpness he needed. Josephine's eyes met Wylers then, and they seemed to smile at him. Was she telegraphing something to him? Or was it a trick of his tired imagination? The uncertainty gnawed at him. At that point, Wyler peeled the corners of his cards an inch off the felt, revealing an ace of hearts and a king of hearts—one of the better hands he had all night. With his stack dwindling, his make-or-break opportunity had come.

"Bet's to you," the dealer said to Barry.

"Five hundred," Barry said, pressing forward a neat stack of chips. Seat two, Cedrick looked at his cards again before tossing them toward the dealer.

"Fold," he said.

Wyler called the five hundred, as did Greg. Mallory folded. Josephine hesitated a moment, then called. The dealer burned the next card off the deck and spread out the flop. A ten of diamonds, a ten of hearts, and a jack of hearts. Barry checked, confirming Wyler's suspicion he probably had nothing. Wyler liked what he saw in front of him.

"A thousand," Wyler said, placing his chips into the pot.

Greg inspected his cards again. He shook his head in disgust and folded. Josephine called, and Barry, as expected, folded. *One left. Knock her out and you're back in this thing.* The dealer burned the next card, then dropped a six of hearts. At the bare minimum, Wyler had a flush. He stayed conservative with his bet.

"A thousand," he said.

Josephine paused and gazed at Wyler, who returned the stare with a playful smile. She called. The dealer burned the last card, then turned up a two of clubs for the river. *No help to anyone.* The dealer looked to Wyler.

"Bet's to you," she said.

He studied the five cards on the table and analyzed the possibilities of what Josephine had. She either had another jack or a ten, for two pair or three of a kind. Or she also had a flush, in which case Wyler had her beat. He was done for if she had pocket jacks, pocket tens, or a jack and a ten. *Would she have slow-played to the end like this if she had the four-of-a-kind or a full house? Try to trap him with a reraise? Maybe. Or she was bluffing since she had the flexibility to do it with her higher chip stack.* He thought of her spinning the ring on her finger. *What did that tell him? What type of hand did she consider worthy of the tell? A queen and jack of hearts? Did she have the lower flush?*

Or did she have one of the pocket pairs? Was the touch of her ring not even a tell? Or was it a mindless habitual thing she did with no meaning behind it? Play it cautious or play it risky? When faced with gray decisions, Wyler struggled with the cautious route. A symptom that plagued him since his youth.

"I'm all in," Wyler said as he carefully counted his chips, then moved the stacks to the center of the pot. The dealer counted them, then spoke to Josephine, "Thirty-two thousand, five hundred."

Josephine stared at the chips, then at the dealer, then finally turned her attention to Wyler. The corner of her lips eased itself into a smile. And Wyler instantly understood he miscalculated. His stomach sank as he waited for the double tap of words to shoot from her mouth.

"I call," Josephine said. She didn't bother pushing her chips forward, for she knew she had won the hand already.

"Call. Cards, please," the dealer said.

Wyler turned his ace and king over and flipped them toward the dealer.

"An ace high flush," the dealer announced.

With the smile still on her face and her eyes on Wyler, Josephine gently handed her cards to the dealer, who laid them on the table.

"Pocket jacks. Full house."

Josephine leaned forward to collect her winnings.

"Nicely done," Wyler said.

"Thank you," Josephine said. "I love a gracious loser."

Wyler grunted and pushed away from the table. The smile never left Josephine's face as she organized his chips amongst her own.

"Tough break, man," Greg said.

"Good playing with you, Declan," Barry chimed in.

"Yeah, yeah. Good luck, everybody," Wyler said, standing. "Come on, Blackjack. Time for a much needed drink."

Wyler took a step to his right, past his canine companion, Blackjack, a male Belgian Malinois. The seventy-pound, tan-bodied, black-faced dog rose and trotted alongside Wyler. Most people considered dogs as ordinary pets. Blackjack, on the other hand, was the furthest thing from one. After Wyler rescued him as a puppy, the two never spent more than a few hours apart. Through rigorous and sometimes experimental training, the pair formed an unbreakable bond.

The duo weaved through the other tables, stopping at the bar against the back wall.

"Hey, Ellie," Wyler said to the bartender.

"You want the usual?" she said, with a sympathetic smile.

"Please. And a bowl and a bottle of water too."

"You got it."

Ellie busied herself with the order. She grabbed a tulip glass and pulled the Guinness tap lever. When the dark ruby-red liquid filled the glass three-quarters of the way, she released the lever. From under the bar, she found a peanut bowl, and placed it and the bottle of water in front of Wyler. Then she returned to the beer and finished filling the remainder of the glass.

"The drink's on me," a man said, placing a fifty-dollar bill on the countertop and sliding it toward Ellie. Wyler turned to see a familiar face. Arlo Riggins stood beside a stool, leaning against a sleek matte black cane. He wore a slim-fit brown tweed suit with a light blue button-down shirt underneath the blazer. Arlo got the cane after losing his foot to an IED blast in Afghanistan when they were in the Marines together years ago. Wyler remembered the sight in vivid detail as if it were yesterday.

Wyler said, "Ellie, I'd like you to meet Arlo Riggins. One of the country's future billionaires."

Arlo smiled with mild embarrassment.

"Billionaire, huh?" Ellie said, smirking. "Are you single?"

"I'm afraid I'm married to the job."

"And what's that?"

"I run a brokerage firm out of New York."

"Ah," Ellie said with practiced interest. "So, you're a gambler too?"

Arlo shrugged. "In a manner of speaking."

"Can I get you something to drink Mr. Future Billionaire?"

"He doesn't drink," Wyler said.

"A Wall Street man that doesn't drink?" Ellie said. "That's new."

Wyler grinned. "If you can believe it, he's actually one of the good ones."

"I didn't know such a thing existed," she said with a playful laugh.

"It is a rarity," Wyler said. "He makes up for it by taking care of dogs. There's still a little hope for him."

"Who doesn't love dogs?" she said.

"He even built a state-of-the-art sanctuary for them."

"A sanctuary?" Ellie said. "Like AA for celebrities?"

"Not quite," Arlo said, smiling. "We take in dogs without a place to go. Dogs that have been beaten or left for dead, and give them a chance at a new life."

"He's underselling it," Wyler said. "A lot of training goes into the dogs living there. Beyond anything anyone else is doing anywhere."

"Like what?" Ellie said as she took the fifty off the bartop.

Wyler looked to Arlo to explain. Arlo took a step forward, and said, "We focus on psychology and advanced techniques in how we communicate with each other. Lately, we've begun exploring sign language."

"You teach dogs that?" she said, opening the register and slipping the bill in.

"We still have a long way to go, but we're making inroads," Arlo said.

"Is that how Blackjack got so smart? He go to this sanctuary of yours?"

Wyler nodded. "For a time."

"Declan helped set up most of the programs with me," Arlo said. "I've never seen someone connect with dogs like him. Almost like he's one of them."

Ellie placed the change on the bar, sliding it to Arlo with a perfectly manicured finger. "Well, Mr. Future Billionaire dog lover, if you ever get a divorce from your job, come look me up."

Ignoring the money, Arlo said, "I just might."

"Have a good night boys," she said, tossing a smile over her shoulder as she moved on to the next gambler looking for comfort at the bottom of a bottle.

Wyler studied the hawk-like features of his friend's face. "So, what brings you to this fine establishment? I'm hoping you came in after I embarrassed myself."

Arlo grinned, and the two friends shook hands. "I always told you numbers are more reliable than your gut. The odds weren't with you on that one."

"Numbers don't account for the whims of the human psyche."

"They would if you'd let them."

Wyler smiled. "What can I say? I'm a lost cause."

Arlo turned his attention to the dog at Wyler's side.

"Hello, Blackjack. It's good to see you. Are you keeping him out of trouble?" Arlo said with a nod toward Wyler.

Blackjack barked once, signaling a yes. The response brought a smile to Arlo's face.

"I never tire of that," Arlo said. "You've kept up with the training, I take it."

Wyler nodded. "He understands a lot. More than some people I've met."

"I can imagine." Arlo reached out a hand, and Blackjack allowed him to scratch behind his ear. A gesture granted to few people. "You and Enola should be proud of what you taught him. He's a magnificent example of what can be achieved."

Looking into his drink, Wyler said, "How is she?"

Arlo shrugged. "Enola? Same as always, I suppose. Brilliant. Hot-tempered. Arrogant. Do I need to continue?"

"No."

"She asks about you."

Wyler smiled. "No, she doesn't."

"Well, I like to believe she thinks about you, at least."

Wyler downed half the Guinness on his first sip. Then he said, "What do you need this time, Arlo? I know you're not here to make small talk with my dog and reminisce about my ex."

"Is there someplace we can sit?"

Wyler drained the rest of the beer, then tilted his head for Arlo to follow him. He navigated the poker room of the Whitmore, turning down a hall that opened into another game parlor. To his right stood a glass wall with a double door centered between its width. The three of them emerged from the doors onto an expansive deck with the glowing lights of the Atlantic City skyline as their backdrop. A handful of circular tables decorated the space.

Four white couches lined the back railing overlooking the ocean. Wyler selected the couch to the far left, providing them with some privacy. He sat on the edge of the couch, and Blackjack settled into a position next to him.

"They don't mind him being in here?" Arlo said, nodding toward Blackjack.

"I made an arrangement with the owner. The guy flew helicopters during Vietnam. Told him I was a dog handler with the Marines. So he made an exception. Private places like this suit us better than the casinos anyway. Fewer tourists and bachelorette parties."

"Tourists are quite unbearable," Arlo said, taking in the nighttime view.

When Wyler settled into the seat, he said, "I'm all ears."

"I've got a job for you."

"I've already got two jobs."

"Well, if you consider gambling one of them, you might need to go back to school."

Wyler grinned. "Too soon, Arlo."

"And what's your other job? Are you still working as security for the casino?"

"It pays the bills and allows me to get into tournaments here and there."

"And you think that's the best use of your and Blackjack's talents? Chasing down the one-in-a-thousand desperate guy who tries to make off with a few hundred bucks of the casino's money. You trained him for war. "

"We search the parking lots, too, if you must know."

"For what?"

"Make sure no one gets robbed walking to their cars. Inspect cars here and there."

"Why?"

"See if anyone planted a bomb under a high roller's car."

"That's happened before?"

"Once, as far as I know."

"And that's all it took for you to get the job?"

Wyler shrugged. "Listen, they asked if Blackjack had explosives training, and I said yes. If it makes them feel better and gives them something to brag about to their high rollers, then who am I to argue. I get paid either way. Plus, it gives Blackjack something to do, and he gets to be with me for the day."

"You were doing more meaningful work at the sanctuary."

"Well, Enola didn't want me there anymore. She saw me as a distraction. So I left. I'm pretty sure you didn't forget all of that."

Arlo sighed and shrugged. "I can't change what happened."

Wanting to get away from the painful memories of his ex, Wyler said, "Tell me what's going on?"

Arlo sat next to Wyler on the couch, holding on to his cane near his knee.

"As the sanctuary has grown over the years, I've established many partnerships with kennels and shelters throughout the country," Arlo said. "They keep me abreast of dogs coming in and out of their organizations. I've also asked them to notify me if anything out of the ordinary ever shows up."

"I'm aware."

"I was talking with a woman at a shelter in Georgia. During our conversation, she asked me if I'd heard about the dog they found at their sister shelter in Alabama. Apparently, five days ago, somebody dropped off a greyhound they'd found half dead in their backyard in the middle of nowhere."

"A greyhound?"

"That's right. The shelter takes the dog in. It won't eat. Won't go to the bathroom. Pretty far gone case, but the doctors believed they could bring her back to a stable degree of health."

"Ok."

"The next morning, the dog's dead."

"That's not that uncommon with strays."

"True, but after they did some blood work, they found traces of cocaine and enough fentanyl in its system to kill about three full-grown men."

"It's the south. Again that's not uncommon."

"They opened the dog up. It had three vials of semi-digested pills in the dog's stomach."

"Maybe the dog lived with a doctor and accidentally got into their stash."

"In the middle of the woods?"

"Could have been with a drug dealer and ate some."

"It's possible, but what would a drug dealer be doing with a greyhound? A pitbull, ok, I might buy. But a greyhound? Not their style of dog. And...in the middle of rural Alabama?"

Wyler considered the point as he stroked Blackjack's neck.

"None of this sounds off to you?" Arlo said.

"I didn't say that."

"So what do you think?"

"About what?"

"Would you be willing to go there and check it out for me? See if it's an isolated incident like you suggest, or find out if something else is going on."

Wyler snorted. "Come on, Arlo."

"What?"

"Do I need to remind you about the last job I did for you?"

"What about it?"

"I'm lucky to be alive or not rotting away in a prison cell."

"Yet here you are, still breathing and not in jail. I'd consider that a success. Plus, you got Blackjack out of it. That does nothing for you?"

Wyler leaned closer to Arlo and lowered his voice. "And what about the bodies I left behind?"

Arlo waved his hand dismissively. "They got what they deserved. You know that better than anyone. I didn't see that type of conscience when we were overseas."

"That was different."

"How?"

Wyler didn't respond.

"A monster's a monster," Arlo said. "As far as I see it, there's no difference."

"And you want me to go so you can keep your distance, right?"

Arlo shrugged. "You know I would go." He tapped his foot with his cane. "This doesn't lend itself to the rough and tumble stuff anymore, unfortunately." He shifted in the seat. "And yes, to your point, if something went left and I got implicated..."

"Yeah, I know. All of your investors, who I'm sure are all morally sound, would run for the hills."

"If there's no money coming in, I'm not much use to helping these animals get a better life."

"What about the cops? Shouldn't they be handling this?"

"If the cops had wanted to help or cared, do you think I'd be here asking you this?"

"You can't save them all, Arlo."

"I have to try, don't I?"

Wyler inhaled deeply through his nose, drawing the cool night air into his chest, then released it from his mouth.

"I don't know," Wyler said.

Arlo quietly rotated the cane in his hands. "How much did you lose tonight?"

"Why?"

"How much?"

"The entry fee cost thirty grand."

"And what would you say you'd earn in a week? On average."

"Depends," Wyler said. "A lot of peaks and valleys exist. Right now, unfortunately, I'm in one of the valleys."

"Ballpark it for me."

"Last week, I pulled in three grand and change from poker and about a grand from the security detail."

"I'll pay you fifty grand for, let's say, at the most two weeks' worth of work."

"Fifty grand?"

"That'll get back your entry fee and cover what you might have earned weekly with, give or take, a twelve thousand add-on. Plus, I'll take care of any of your expenses. Food, hotels...whatever you need."

Wyler's eyebrow arched with interest. "Half up front? Cash?"

"Sure."

Wyler grinned. If Arlo had an animal counterpart, it would be some sort of bird of prey.

"Do you ever get tired of being a crusader?" Wyler asked.

"Do you ever get tired of making me debase myself to get you to do something I know you're going to do anyway?"

"Not really."

"So, you'll do it?"

"I've got a shift in an hour. Give me a day to think about it."

"I'm going to hold you to that," Arlo said. He used his cane to pull himself to an upright position. "Twenty-four hours. You've got my number. Let me know one way or the other."

"I will."

Arlo shook Wyler's hand. "Good to see you. Always a pleasure, Blackjack." He patted the dog on the head, and then he walked back into the Whitmore.

Once Arlo was gone, Wyler turned to Blackjack.

"What?"

Blackjack glanced at Wyler, then looked away.

"What? You're telling me you think this is a good idea?"

Blackjack continued to avoid eye contact with Wyler.

"You think we should do it?"

Blackjack barked once.

"So you're going to take his side? I'm trying to keep us safe. Keep you safe."

Blackjack ignored him.

"You're a piece of work," Wyler said as he stood. "Come on, we've got a job to do right now."

Blackjack didn't move as Wyler headed for the exit.

"Really? You're going to play it like that, huh? Let's go. Stop messing around."

Blackjack stayed in place. Wyler walked back to the dog and crouched in front of him.

"You know this isn't going to be as simple as he's making it out to be."

Wyler stared at Blackjack, then he went to the rail, and peered into the night. After five minutes, he sighed as he pulled out his phone and called Arlo.

Chapter 3

A black Range Rover SV idled in the parking lot behind the Whitmore. Arlo settled into the plush leather back seat when his phone rang. He smiled as he read the name on the screen of his phone and answered on the fourth ring.

"That was fast," Arlo said.

"I want thirty grand in cash upfront," Wyler said. "I'll text you where to leave it. If you can get the money by tomorrow morning, then you've got yourself a deal."

"That can be arranged."

"I'm not promising anything. You need to limit your expectations of what I find. If I think whatever this is, is a one-off incident, I need to know you'll be ok with that."

"That's fair."

"And I get paid either way?"

"Yes."

"And I need assurance if something goes wrong, I won't be

left in the breeze."

"You weren't before."

"That was then, this is now."

"How soon could you leave?"

After a brief pause, Wyler said, "I've got to square things with my boss at the casino, but I should be able to head out tomorrow."

"Ok, I'll send you all the information I have and the contact to meet up with once you're there."

"Alright."

"You're doing a good thing."

"For my wallet, I am."

"That's the only reason?"

Wyler didn't respond.

Arlo laughed. "I didn't think so. Good luck, Declan."

Wyler tucked the phone into his pocket and then looked at Blackjack.

"Are you happy now?"

Blackjack barked once.

"Let's go. We've got some packing to do."

As they headed home, Wyler called his boss at the casino. When Wyler told him he needed at least a week off, his boss laid on a guilt trip but eventually relented. With work squared away, they continued the mile walk back to their apartment nestled in the city's eastern section. The complex was built in the 1920s, and its exterior displayed that fact. Worn beige bricks, with sections of red gave it the texture of a patchwork quilt. The building reached three stories and housed forty units. Wyler and Blackjack lived on the third floor with a barely there view of the ocean. They entered the two-bedroom apartment. The interior was dated, but Wyler had transformed the place into a cozy bachelor pad after a coat of paint and some modern appliances.

The living room consisted of a long sleek gray fabric couch and a matching seat and ottoman set. A rectangular mahogany coffee table adorned with a slew of books on Texas Hold 'em sat in front of the couch. A wide-screen TV with a layer of dust coating the screen occupied the opposite wall. He turned on a lamp in the bedroom. Aside from Wyler's bed and the nightstand, nothing else filled the room. All of the clothes he owned fit inside the small bedroom closet. Wyler kicked off his boots and placed them neatly to the side of the nightstand. Then he made his way to the second bedroom that served as his office and gear storage space. A matching mahogany desk with an iMac on top rested in front of a window. Two substantial utility cabinets filled the right-hand wall. Wyler unlatched and pulled down a wood slab on the left wall that functioned as a workbench.

From the closet, he removed a tan tactical 35L backpack with a plethora of pockets. He placed it on the workbench, then went to the first utility cabinet. He punched in the six-digit code on the keypad, unlocking the doors. Gear of all shape, size, and use, neatly stocked the cabinet's interior. The first item he slid into the backpack was his reliable MacBook. Then he worked through a mental checklist of the items he knew were always good to have. A pair of compact binoculars, night vision goggles, and a night vision monocular went into the pack next. Two portable battery packs followed, along with a TOPS Brakimo field knife and a first aid kit loaded with the essentials to treat cuts or bullet wounds. He placed a water filtration kit inside a small camp stove and stuffed it into the bag with a 40 oz. stainless steel water bottle. The last two items he selected were a flashlight and a USB-powered lantern. He closed the doors and then opened the second utility cabinet.

He spun the dial of a compact safe bolted to the top shelf. Out of it, he took a minimalist wallet that contained a fake ID and a credit card linked to one of Arlo's hidden accounts. The fake ID spawned from the first job Wyler undertook for him. They both agreed a layer of protection to hide who they were was a logical safety precaution. He closed the safe and then relocked the cabinet. The rest of his stuff he left to pack in the morning.

In the kitchen, he turned on a speaker on top of the fridge. He selected a blues playlist on his phone. *My Mind Is Rambling,* a Black Keys cover of the Junior Kimbrough song played. As the gritty guitar and drums filled the space, Wyler prepared dinner. He set a cast iron skillet on the stove to heat up. While it did, he grabbed a packet of ground bison from the fridge, forming it into two patties. When the skillet was hot, he dropped the burgers in with a satisfying sizzle, then cracked some salt and pepper over them. As the bison cooked, he peeled and chopped two sweet potatoes into fries, seasoned them, and threw them in the oven. He turned the skillet heat to low until the fries finished baking. From the cabinet, he grabbed two plates and divided the food into equal portions.

It was a simple meal, his favorite kind. The kind of meal he learned to make as a kid on the nights his parents were on a gambling streak and he was left to take care of himself. The fewer the ingredients, the fewer things could go wrong. His selections gravitated toward foods with an inherent good taste that only required minimal seasoning. He limited the meals to one type of meat with one type of starch or vegetable to accompany it. The pared down cooking style set his expectations low for what a meal should be. If it kept him alive, then the meal was a success.

The mentality served him well when he enlisted in the Marines. His fellow soldiers hated eating MREs, but with Wyler's criteria, the packets of food didn't phase him in the least.

Wyler poured himself a Guinness and set the meal on the table. Blackjack sat next to him and waited patiently for his dinner. Wyler placed the plate at his paws and said, "Eat."

Blackjack tore into the burger and polished it off in seconds, and the fries disappeared shortly after. As part of their meal-time ritual, Wyler dumped a basket of toys, close to forty total, onto the floor in the living room and then sat down to eat. After swallowing a bite of the burger, he said, "Chicken."

Blackjack darted over to the pile of real-life-looking toys and rummaged through them until he found the chicken. He picked it up in his mouth and deposited it in the empty basket next to Wyler.

"Good boy," Wyler said. "Car."

Back into the pile Blackjack went. The game lasted under half an hour, with Blackjack correctly selecting all but two of the designated toys. As he dropped in the last one, a pistol, Wyler pet his head and said, "Nice work." After the last bite of fries and gulp of beer, Wyler cleaned the dishes and then got ready for bed. Wearing only his boxers, he slipped under the welcoming sheets. Blackjack took to his position at the foot of the bed. Wyler closed his eyes and focused on his breathing. He worked the 4-7-8 technique, which consisted of breathing in through his nose for four seconds, holding his breath for seven seconds, and then exhaling for eight seconds. Among other things, it was introduced to him by his ex. Her voice drifted into his mind as if she was laying next to him. "Breathe in," she said. "Hold. Now release." The steadiness of her voice reduced the occurrence of his night terrors. Whatever heartbreak lingered from Enola, he remained grateful to her for bringing this element into his life. By the tenth cycle of the breath work, he was out cold.

To stave off some of the effects of the long trip ahead, Wyler woke at six the next morning. He threw on a pair of gym shorts, a t-shirt, and sneakers, then took Blackjack for a three-mile jog on the beach. During his cool down period, Wyler waded into the cold water of the Atlantic, and stared out at the rising sun. With a new mission ahead of him, his mind drifted to the two dogs he lost in combat over his three tour deployment. Instead of pushing the memories aside, Wyler replayed them in detail. He didn't want to forget his partners, or what they sacrificed. Ever. For each of the dog's lives, they had saved dozens of his brothers in arms. Wyler clung to the pain he felt after losing his first dog, Thunder, to a suicide bomber barricaded in a fortified compound. He could still feel the concussion from the explosion against his chest. The bomb had left Wyler with nothing of the dog to even bury. His memories continued to his second dog, Reno, who bled out in his hands after a piece of shrapnel severed a major artery in his leg. As the dog faded, Wyler poured words from his heart, words he'd never uttered to another person, not even Enola.

He turned toward Blackjack then, who meandered a few feet back out of the tide's range. The dog was smart, probably the smartest one Wyler ever worked with. Blackjack responded well to training, and showed expert level skill in tracking, detection, and obedience. *But was he ready for a job like this?* Wyler trained him like he would have any other military dog, plus he had the extra benefits of Enola's psychological regimen. Training though, was different than the real thing. When he analyzed all the aspects of the dog's life, Wyler trusted the creature implicitly. And for what they were about to embark on, no other option existed. If there was doubt, it could get them both killed.

"Come here," Wyler said, emerging from the water. He crouched down to pet Blackjack as he came to Wyler's side. "Good boy." Wyler didn't know what he'd find in Alabama, but whatever it was, he needed to prepare himself mentally for the possibility of something happening to Blackjack. Each dog that died on his watch, Wyler lost a piece of himself. Every death hurt. Every death mattered. They had to; otherwise, what was the point? The idea of helping someone or some creature to live one more day kept Wyler going. Gave him a shred of meaning. It was a fine line putting Blackjack's life in harm's way for some random dogs. If Wyler didn't try to help, his complacency would eat away at him the rest of his life.

"Let's go," Wyler said.

When they returned to the apartment, Wyler knocked out two sets of fifty pushups, two sets of ten pull-ups, and two sets of fifty crunches. With his exercise finished, Wyler cooked breakfast. He scrambled six eggs and poured them into a skillet filled with corned beef hash. One half of the mixture went onto a plate, and the other half he dumped into a bowl for Blackjack. A tall glass of orange juice and a cup of black coffee accompanied Wyler's meal.

When they finished eating, Wyler washed the dishes and tidied the apartment. In the bathroom, he shaved but left his thick, evenly-trimmed mustache alone. He grabbed an ancient pair of clippers from a drawer, set it to the lowest setting, and buzzed his head. When on a mission, he wanted the least amount of care needed for personal grooming. After he swept the shorn hair from the floor, he hopped in the shower. Two minutes of hot water, then two minutes of cold. He toweled off and dressed in a fresh pair of jeans and a white t-shirt layered under a gray sweatshirt.

In a tan canvas duffle bag, he stuffed a few clothing and toiletry essentials. Since Arlo planned to cover incidentals, Wyler figured he could buy anything else as the need arose. Wyler laced up a set of well-traveled boots, then slid on a khaki-colored bomber jacket. He patted the coat pockets, double checking that his custom-made tungsten carbide knuckledusters were inside—a weapon he rarely left the house without. Many of his military buddies prodded him to carry a handgun, which he wasn't opposed to, but for Wyler, guns sometimes created more complications than they were worth. From the scrapes he'd been in over the years, he found a heavy piece of metal slamming into someone's face ended any heated conversation.

Wyler tossed some dried food—jerky, trail mix, and some apples—into the duffle bag and zipped it. He filled a two-gallon jug of water, then did a final sweep of the apartment until he was satisfied everything was in order. Returning to a messy home bothered him since he was a kid. He threw on the backpack of gear, slung the duffle bag over his shoulder, and then held the door open for Blackjack to exit.

Outside, they walked a block to the east, stopping at a three-floor parking garage. Near the gated entrance, Wyler stepped into a cramped office. A short heavyset man with bushy gray hair sat behind a counter, reading a magazine. He peered at Wyler over a set of thin reading glasses. When he realized who it was, he quickly tossed aside the magazine and stood.

"Declan, my man. How are you today? It's been a while."

"I'm good, Don. How about you?"

"Well," Don said, removing his glasses. "My daughter agreed

to let me come see her new baby. So, things are looking up."

"I told you with time, she'd come around."

"That you did. That you did."

"Did a package come for me this morning?" Wyler said, not wanting to give Don an opportunity to relive his sordid past of drinking, womanizing, and gambling that left his life in ruins.

"Yes," Don said, crouching behind the counter. "A skinny-looking guy dropped this off for you." Don handed Wyler a small brown box.

"Thanks," Wyler said, turning to leave. Over his shoulder, he said to Don, "And bring a gift for your grandkid. Don't scrimp either."

"I will." Don waved. "Don't be a stranger."

Wyler and Blackjack climbed the stairs to the second floor. Along the inside wall of the garage, where the exit ramp sliced through it, rested a 1978 Ford Bronco with a rust-colored exterior. A purchase from a summer when he'd hit a hot streak at the tables, leaving him with money to burn. He overhauled the vehicle top to bottom, converting it to electric power, and all the modern automotive conveniences on the market. Aware driving was his primary mode of transportation, Wyler had the back seat removed and replaced with a solid floor to use as a place for him and Blackjack to sleep.

Wyler opened the driver's side door, and Blackjack leaped into the cab, settling into his place in the passenger seat. In the back, Wyler stored their few supplies in a concealed compartment beneath the bed floor. He climbed in behind the wheel. From the console, he grabbed a Swiss Army knife and cut open the brown box. Inside lay a black safe with a keypad on the front. A note on top read, *Code is the day you found Blackjack. Good luck. -A.* Wyler punched in the six-digit code, and the safe door clicked open. Blocks of crisp hundred-dollar bills filled the interior. If there was one thing about Arlo, it was that he was a man of his word. Wyler counted out fifteen thousand dollars. He pulled a white envelope from the glove box, stuffed the cash inside, sealed it, and then placed it in his jacket's pocket. After that, he counted two thousand dollars, folded it in half, and slid the cash into his pants pocket. The remainder of the money he returned to the safe. He opened a hidden compartment beneath Blackjack's seat and placed the black box inside.

"Ok," Wyler said. "Let's get you buckled in."

Wyler helped Blackjack into his custom-made safety harness—a precaution if they were ever in collision. The harness tethered to a beam behind the seat cushion. A specially designed pressure release system connected the harness to the tether. Blackjack could simply bite down on the connector, freeing him from the seat.

"Comfortable?" Wyler said.

Blackjack barked once.

"Alright then, we have to make one quick stop, then we're on the road."

Wyler scratched Blackjack's chest, then started the SUV. He maneuvered out of the garage and eased into the flow of traffic. After a thirty-five minute drive, Wyler pulled into the lot of the Green Pines Retirement Homes. Before getting out, Wyler closed his eyes and took two deep breaths, fortifying himself for what he might see in the next few minutes. He opened his eyes and looked at Blackjack.

"Are you coming?"

Blackjack barked twice, *no.*

"Coward." Wyler grumbled.

He rolled down the windows, then got out. In the reception area of the main building, Wyler approached a smiling middle-aged woman.

"Hi, is Bethany in?" Wyler said.

"Do you know someone who lives here?"

"Yes."

"Let me see if she's available. What's your name?"

"Declan Wyler. She knows me."

"One second."

The woman picked up her phone and pressed a few buttons. "Hi, Bethany. A Mr. Wyler is here to see you." She listened briefly, then hung up. "She'll be right out."

Five minutes later, Bethany Frume, the facility director, greeted Wyler. She was tall with dark skin and short hair. A gray pantsuit with a vibrant floral patterned blouse highlighted the figure of a classy older woman. Her smile always had a way of putting Wyler at ease.

"Nice to see you again, Declan."

Wyler nodded. "Bethany."

"What can I do for you?" she said, holding her arm out and leading them down a hallway.

"I'm going to be out of town for a little bit. At least a week. It could be longer. I just wanted someone to know in case she forgets what I tell her today."

"Of course. I'll make a note of it."

"And I've got this for you as well," Wyler said, extracting the cash envelope from his jacket. "Apologies it's a little late, but that should cover things for her for the next couple of months."

Without opening the envelope, Bethany nodded graciously.

"Thank you."

"So, how has she been?"

"We've noted a decline in her cognition which is fairly standard. In the mornings, she's usually at her best and clearest. Her memories tend to get foggy and jumbled as the day wears on."

"She hasn't hit anyone again, has she?"

"No. Thankfully that appears to have been an isolated incident."

"Good."

Bethany stopped at a door. "Are you going anywhere nice?"

"Not particularly," Wyler said.

She lightly tapped her knuckles on the door. "Mrs. Wyler, you have a visitor."

After a moment of silence, a muffled voice said, "It's open."

"It was nice seeing you," Bethany said. "Safe travels."

Wyler nodded and then opened the door. The studio apartment consisted of a narrow kitchen flanked by a couch and a TV in the living room. A twin bed burrowed into the corner of the room. Sitting at a table in front of an open window, Wyler's mother pruned a plant. He put a hand on her shoulder and kissed her cheek.

"How are you doing, mom?"

She leaned back in her chair, staring at him.

"Liam, when did you get here?" she said.

"It's me, mom, Declan. Dad's been gone for ten years."

She continued to stare at him with a blank expression, then she broke out laughing.

"I know," she said, composing herself. "I got you good. You should see your face."

"You shouldn't joke about that here. If one of these people takes you seriously, they'll lock you up with the people who crap their pants."

"Oh, stop. When did you become so serious?"

Wyler sighed. "I don't know."

"Did you bring me some cigarettes, at least?"

"I've already told you they don't want you smoking."

"Christ, can't a woman live the way she wants to live with the few years she's got left?"

"The short answer is no."

"Ah, you're no fun," she said, waving a hand at Wyler and returning to her pruning. "So to what do I owe this unexpected visit?"

"I'm going away, but I'm not sure for how long. A few days, maybe two weeks. Just wanted to let you know. If you really need to get in touch with me, tell Bethany."

"You headed to Iraq or Afghanistan?"

"I... I'm not in the service anymore..." Wyler paused. "Are you messing with me again?"

She grinned and shrugged her shoulders.

Wyler shook his head. "You're evil."

She shrugged again as she snipped a dying petal.

"I'm going to put a reminder on your fridge," Wyler said.

"I'm fine," she said with a huff, slapping her shears to the table. "Go ahead and test me. Let me run a count."

"Mom..."

"Go ahead. I know you carry those cards with you wherever you go. Give me five hands, plus the dealer. I'll be spot on."

Wyler considered her for a moment, knowing arguing wouldn't get him far. He reached into his jacket and brought out a deck of playing cards. Black ink covered the case, and the Marine Corps emblem sat dead center. A going-away gift from his dad before he shipped out for basic training. The day Wyler's dad gave him the cards was the last day he saw him alive.

Wyler shuffled the deck, dealt six cards up in one pass, and did another six in the second pass. His mom's eyes flickered over the pairs of blackjack hands. In his head, he counted to five, then dealt the remaining cards for each hand based on how someone would call them as if they were at a real table. When all the hands were played out, he counted a generous ten seconds and then collected the cards.

"Well?" he said.

She stared at the table as if the cards were still there. As she struggled to tally the count, her pupils dilated with hopelessness that broke his heart. She picked up her shears, turning away from Wyler. The jocularity faded from her face. She clipped another petal, then whispered. "Negative one."

The count was plus three, but Wyler couldn't bring himself to tell her otherwise.

"You got it," he said.

As an on-again, off-again blackjack dealer and accomplice with his dad, Wyler's mom—in her prime—counted cards at a blackjack table as easily as breathing. He remembered seeing her keep a running count for three hours straight, which made what he witnessed much more painful.

"I've got a long drive ahead of me. I should get going," Wyler said, standing, trying to keep the melancholy from his voice.

"Ok," she said.

He kissed her on the cheek again and said, "You behave."

"Yeah, yeah," she said with a faint smile.

Wyler stopped at the kitchen and glanced over his shoulder. His mom kept her attention on the plant. He crept to the fridge and wrote a reminder message on the dry-erase board that he was leaving for a while. At the door, he took one last look behind him, and then he was gone.

Chapter 4

Clayton's hands probed through the darkness of his dream. A cacophony of barking dogs surrounded him, steadily growing louder. He tried to escape but his legs were sunk in a thick sludge. The barking turned into growls and drowned out any other sound. A curdled wetness hung on the growls like the creatures were drowning in blood. Then one of the dogs leaped from the void and hit him in the chest, snarling and full of hate. Clayton's hands shot out and clamped around the dog's neck. He squeezed in a terrified rage. Shadows careened across the dog. Half its face lacked fur and skin, revealing a pulsing mess of sinew and bone. A hot stickiness seeped between his fingers. More terrified, Clayton squeezed harder, screaming into the dog's face. The pressure he applied dislodged the dog's left eyeball from its socket. Despite this, the dog's foaming mouth kept moving. Kept trying to tear Clayton to pieces. To devour him along with his soul.

Using the last of his strength, Clayton dug his fingers in, forming a fist. The motion severed the creature's head from its torso. And to his horror, the dog's mouth continued to snap at him with more ferocity. Then teeth sunk into his legs, thighs, arms, and neck. The mutilated pack of dogs descended on him like a wave. He released a final scream, which carried him from the realm of dreams back to reality. Clayton tumbled from his bed to the floor, thrashing as if he were still fighting off the dogs. Fully awake, he rolled to his back, struggling to catch his breath. His skin dripped with sweat. He staggered to his feet and stumbled into the bathroom, where he proceeded to dry heave into the toilet. The porcelain bowl cooled his boiling skin.

As nausea passed and his heart rate slowed, he got to his feet and ambled down the hallway. He turned left, down another short corridor, entering the kitchen. Through a side door, he went outside. The morning air was warm and laced with humidity. He paced the lawn attempting to shake the unsettling dream. It left him anxious about what the day would bring. He stared at the squat single-story house his grandfather had built. The last storm had done a number on the place. Two shutters were missing along with strips of siding. A section of the gutters lay bent on the ground, half buried in the long since dead flower beds. The windows had a layer of grime on them Clayton could never fully get rid of. A blue tarp fluttered gently on the roof, covering a fist sized hole he didn't have the money to fix.

Clayton was the third generation of the Judge line to inherit the place. A burden to carry with a dwindling list of redeeming qualities. The house was located on a large tract of land near the Apalachicola National Forest in the northwest section of Florida. No other houses existed within a fifteen-mile radius. Its isolation and nearly an hour's drive to the nearest beach made the place a challenge to sell, which Clayton had tried on multiple occasions. When realtors learned Clayton's grandfather died in the house, few realtors accepted the challenge of taking the listing. Resigned to the hard truth that no one would buy the place, and not having much going on in his life at the time, Clayton moved in.

The more he breathed in the fresh air, the calmer he got. Clayton walked across the front yard toward the massive pond that occupied a chunk of land. Cutting around the back side of the pond was the one main road leading to civilization. He walked into the pond, up to his shins. The tepid water aided in regulating his overheated system. He closed his eyes and tried to visualize his future, where he was free from his father's sins and the people making him pay for them. *Buy time, stick to the plan,* he told himself, *and you've got a chance.* His eyes opened at the faint sound of barking. He left the pond and headed to the shed off to the side of the house. Inside, the lights scattered the darkness, revealing a packed space of caged greyhounds.

"Shut up." Clayton shouted.

He stomped past the cages, kicking at any of the ones with nonsubmissive dogs standing. For those that didn't respond to his commands, he blasted them in the face with a home-brewed low-grade pepper spray. He smiled as the dogs then recoiled in fear. After tossing their meager helping of food into their cages, he killed the lights and slammed the shed door behind him.

Feeling better, he strolled back to the house. Jed stood at the stove cooking something, as Clayton entered the kitchen. Jed wore a pair of ratty shorts and a loose—equally ratty—tank top. Clayton looked at his lanky cousin, who had come to live with him after his recent stint in prison for stealing catalytic converters. The police liked him as the prime suspect for a separate incident involving a carjacking that went wrong, leaving the driver dead from multiple stab wounds. Clayton remembered sitting across from his cousin at the prison. Him pleading to Clayton to help him beat the murder charge.

"Listen, they don't have solid evidence on me that I stabbed the guy," Jed had said. "All you have to say is I was with you that night, working at the track, and I'll beat the rap. I promise. Otherwise, I'm looking at life or the death penalty."

Clayton didn't particularly care for his cousin, but if he helped him, Jed would be indebted to him forever. And that had its uses. Clayton forged paperwork stating Jed was a contract worker at the track. He then doctored time cards to coincide with the stabbing, and even lied under oath that Jed was with him the night of the murder, miles from where it occurred. Jed ended up getting off the murder charge, but still had to serve time for stealing the catalytic converters. When Jed's two years were up, with no place else to go, he arrived on Clayton's doorstep, ready to die for the man who'd saved his life.

"I'm making some eggs and grits," Jed said. "You want some?"

"Not hungry," Clayton said as he moved to the coffee pot.

"Are you alright? I thought I heard you puking."

"I'm fine."

"These grits will straighten you right out. You sure you don't want some?"

"I don't want any fucking grits. Thanks."

Jed shrugged. "Suit yourself."

As Clayton was about to sit at the table with his coffee, the distinct sound of a car door closing came through the open living room windows.

"Someone here?" Jed said, turning off the knobs to the oven.

Clayton set the coffee cup down, walked through the connecting corridor, and turned left into the expansive living room. From behind a curtain, he peeked out the window. An expensive black SUV was parked in the driveway, twenty yards from the house. Clayton counted four men coming towards the front door. Three of the guys were big, wearing loose modern polyester pants that tapered at the ankle, like they'd come from the gym. Black t-shirts curved tightly over their muscles. Their hair trimmed short with the sheen of styling gel glistening in the morning sun. When Clayton recognized the man in the center of the group, he hustled back to the kitchen.

"It's them," he said, trying to control the panic in his voice.

"Who?" Jed asked.

"Enzo and three of his guys."

"Ok. Why are you all worked up?"

"Are you joking?"

"Listen, I've dealt with people like Enzo before. It'll be fine if you're straight with him and tell the truth about what happened. They're reasonable people at the end of the day. It's business to them."

"Jesus Christ. Reasonable? How reasonable were guys like that in prison? Reasonable. Whatever you do, please don't fucking talk. Let me handle it."

"I'll let this do the talking," Jed said, pulling a snub-nose revolver out from his waistband hidden beneath his tank top. "If they try to fuck with us, they'll eat a .38."

"What the fuck are you doing with that?" Clayton growled and snatched the gun from his cousin's hand. "Do you want them to kill us today?"

"How do you know that's not what they're planning on

doing anyway?"

"I don't, but let's not give them any more reason to."

"We need to let them know we're not some bitch ass punks. That's what prison taught me."

"What you need to do is shut up and sit there," Clayton said, hiding the revolver in a bucket under the sink.

A knock came at the front door.

"Not a word," Clayton said, pointing his finger threateningly at Jed, who mimed zipping his lips. They walked to the living room, and then Clayton opened the door.

Enzo Crippa stood between two bodyguards. He was dressed in slim white slacks, leather loafers, and a colorful short-sleeve button-down shirt decorated with a pattern of flamingos. A white fedora completed the look. Clayton greeted the respected lieutenant of the Toro crime family with a nod.

"Enzo," he said.

"How are we, boys?" Enzo said.

One of the guards at Enzo's side pushed past Clayton, moving into the house, scanning for any threats before waving Enzo in. The men moved into the living room that hadn't entertained visitors in years. The three guards fanned out through the area, blocking any avenues of escape.

"We're finishing up breakfast. Can I get you guys anything?" Clayton said.

"No, that's not necessary. We won't be staying long," Enzo said.

Clayton held out his hand for them to take a seat. Enzo sank into one of the two chairs angled across from the couch, where Clayton sat. Jed leaned against the wall next to the couch inside the perimeter of bodyguards, eying each of them, and attempting to project strength.

As Enzo adjusted himself in the chair, he removed his hat and set it on the coffee table between them. Clayton forced his muscles to relax. He waited for Enzo to start the conversation. As the silence settled into the room, Clayton's confidence faded. *Was Enzo waiting for him to say something? Why wasn't he talking? It had been a week since their trial run in the woods. Things hadn't gone entirely to plan. That was why he was here, wasn't it?*

As the seconds ticked away in silence, Clayton struggled to decipher what was happening. When the quiet rose to an unbearable level, Clayton said, "Is there a problem?"

Enzo stared at Clayton for what felt to him like a full minute. Then he spoke.

"Well, Clayton, that's what I'm trying to figure out. Our associates in Alabama informed me one of the dogs didn't make it to them. They think you're trying to hold out on us, and you're lying about one of the dogs escaping into the woods."

"That's bullshit." Jed blurted out.

Enzo glanced at Jed, then at the guard closest to him. The guard understood the silent instruction from his boss and lashed out with a striking backhand, catching Jed hard across the side of his face.

"Jesus," Jed said, rubbing his face in surprise.

"Is what they're saying bullshit?" Enzo said to Clayton.

Clayton hesitated, glaring at Jed, then said, "That's not what happened. We brought four dogs. I released each of them myself. I'll swear on that. But if one of them did get lost, there's no chance of that dog surviving or having it tied to us or you in any way. Next time, we'll leash them to the ATV."

"You're assuming there is a next time," Enzo said.

"Why wouldn't there be? Aside from the one dog, which won't

happen again, the setup worked. The product made its way over, no one crossed state lines, and everyone's ass stayed covered. It still provides you with a high level of security, unlike any other transportation methods. So, yeah, why wouldn't there be a next time?"

"Don't get snippy with me," Enzo said. "It was your father who borrowed money from us. It was your father who sunk it all into a failing business venture. It was your father who couldn't pay back his debt. And it was your father who blew his brains out like a coward to get out of what he owed."

Enzo leaned forward, and pointed at Clayton like he was tapping the 'Close Doors' button on an elevator. "Your father put this burden on you. Not me. I'm the one who's giving you a fucking chance here to make things right." He stopped pointing, and shrugged. "Mr. Toro told me you guys weren't worth the hassle anymore. When your track closed, and the laundering stopped, he said we'd never see another dime from you. He wanted me to put a bullet between your eyes and be done with it. Leave your dead body in the gutters for everyone to see what happens when debts aren't honored."

Enzo relaxed back into the chair, grinning. "But I told him, this guy Clayton, I see something in him. Something clever behind those eyes. Give him a chance, and he'll come up with a way to keep himself alive. That's what I told him. And you did, didn't you? So save the attitude for someone else."

Clayton didn't enjoy the trip down memory lane and fought to control his temper from flaring.

"Are you shutting the operation down then, or what?" Clayton said.

Enzo picked at the edge of one of his fingernails. Then he

chuckled and pulled a flask from his shirt pocket.

"You mind if I drink?" Enzo said. "I found this rum while I was in the Caribbean, and I can't get enough of the stuff."

Clayton said nothing. Enzo sipped from the flask, then returned it to his pocket.

"Here's the way I see it," Enzo said. "You've got the green light to keep going, but under the condition there's no more fuck ups, no more lost dogs, or missing product. If I get a call from the other side there is the slightest issue, then it's over, and so are both of you. Do you understand me?"

"I understand."

"And what about this halfbreed?" Enzo said, nodding at Jed. "Does he understand?"

Before Jed could respond, Clayton said, "He gets it."

"For your sake, I hope he does."

Clayton wiped his sweating hands on his pants and started to stand.

"Where are you going?" Enzo said.

"We're not done here?"

"We still haven't covered what you owe now for losing some of our product. Did you think we would say, *oh well, no big deal?*"

The guards snickered as they inched farther into the room. Clayton sank back into the couch with an unease filling his stomach.

"If we had anything to pay you with, we would've done it already," Clayton said.

"I realize that."

"So, what, are you just going to add it to our tab? What's the difference at this point?"

"No, that's not what I had in mind," Enzo said. "If I did that, it doesn't carry much weight. That's not a teachable consequence for what happens when you fuck up."

"Ok..." Clayton glanced at the guards closing in like a snare. His eyes quickly scanned the room for an exit. He could get to the window, but the guards would be on him in seconds.

"Since you lost something of ours that we'll never get back, you, then, need to lose something you'll never get back," Enzo said.

Two guards grabbed Jed's arms and twisted them behind his back. Jed cursed as the guards slammed him to the ground, pressing his face into the dusty wood. Clayton sprang from the couch, watching helplessly as the scene unfolded.

"What the fuck are you doing?" he shouted.

Enzo stayed seated, unphased. The third guard unsheathed a thin knife that looked like it was used for gutting fish. He knelt down and placed his palm on the side of Jed's face, and brought the blade to the base of Jed's ear.

"Get off of me." Jed yelled, rocking side to side in a futile attempt to break free.

"Through Mr. Toro's business dealings, I met this guy from Cuba," Enzo said, talking to Clayton but staring at Jed. "He was some old-school head of something or other for Castro. He told me he liked to cut people's ears off to send a message. Fingers were effective but hidden easier. A missing ear, though, it's a bit more challenging."

"Leave him alone," Clayton said. "You made your point."

"Do you have something else you can give me?"

"Clayton." Jed pleaded.

"Or would you like to take his place?" Enzo said.

Clayton stood frozen, his mind flooded with panic. He sure as hell didn't want to trade places. And as much of an idiot as his cousin was, he didn't deserve the punishment.

"Go ahead," Enzo said to the guard with the knife.

"Clayton." Jed screamed as the curved steel severed a centimeter of flesh at Jed's earlobe. The screams echoed off the room's bare walls, hitting Clayton from every angle.

"Stop," Clayton said.

The knife didn't stop. It made a full inch of progress. Jed thrashed and whimpered, tears streaking over his nose.

"Stop." Clayton repeated.

"Wait," Enzo said to the guard, slicing through Jed's flesh. The knife finally halted. A trail of blood seeped down Jed's face, mixing into his tears.

"I'll move up the timeline," Clayton said. "You initially gave me a year to work off the rest of the debt. Make it six months. I'll make more trips with more dogs and more product. I need him, though." Clayton nodded at Jed. "All of him. To make it work."

"See? A creative thinker," Enzo said. He pulled out his flask and took another sip. "But you'll do it in one month now." Enzo scratched his head, thinking. "Eighty dogs. You run that much product across and you're off the hook. If you don't want me to go back to Mr. Toro with a souvenir, then it needs to be a convincing alternative. And eighty dogs' worth of product in one month, I think could do it. Because frankly, I don't see him having the patience to wait six months. A year was already pushing it."

"A month," Clayton said. "That's tight."

"Well, he can keep sawing away if that's easier."

Jed bucked under the guard in a futile attempt to free himself, cursing through clenched teeth.

Clayton sighed in resignation. "A month. Eighty dogs. We'll get it done."

"Ok," Enzo said. He nodded at the guard with the knife. The guard stood, wiped the blood from the blade on the back of Jed's shirt, then sheathed the knife. The other two guards released Jed's arms and stepped away from him. Jed stayed flat on the floor, cupping his bloodied ear with his hand. Enzo donned his hat as he rose from the chair.

"We'll set up a weekly delivery of the product," Enzo said. "One of the boys here will give you a pickup location on Monday. You bring ten dogs to get loaded. Then deliver on Tuesday to the Bama Boys. If all goes well, we'll load another ten dogs on Wednesday, then you drop off on Thursday. If there's no fuckups, then you move on to the next week until you're done."

Enzo glanced at Jed, then at Clayton. "And since you vouched for smart mouth here, you two are both tied to this now. Understand?" He turned, and the three guards followed him out of the house. Clayton didn't move for three seconds, then he walked to the door and slammed it shut. At the window, peeked out to ensure they were leaving. When the men climbed into the SUV and reversed in the driveway to leave, he looked at Jed.

"You alright?" Clayton said.

Jed turned his bloody and snot-caked face towards Clayton as he rose to a seated position. His face a haze of shock. From the faint putrid smell wafting to Clayton's nose, he guessed Jed pissed his pants.

"So, you still think these guys are reasonable?" Clayton said. Jed peeled his hand away from his ear and gingerly probed the wound. Clayton grabbed a dish rag from the kitchen and threw it to his cousin. Then he said, "Clean yourself up. We've got work to do."

Chapter 5

On the third morning of Wyler's drive south, Blackjack woke him by pawing at his leg. Wyler rubbed the sleep from his eyes. He sat up in his sleeping bag in the back of the Bronco.

"I'm awake," Wyler said. "You got to go?"

Blackjack barked once. Wyler opened the back gate of the SUV, and Blackjack jumped out. Wyler lay down a moment longer, listening to the birds sing at the Shoal Creek Campground outside Atlanta. Fully clothed, Wyler slipped out of his sleeping bag. He stuffed the bag into a compression sack, then put it into the storage compartment under the floor. Wyler preferred sleeping in the vehicle instead of hotels whenever it was feasible. The solitude of nature brought him comfort, and a respite from the Atlantic City crowds. It wasn't that he disliked being around people, he just enjoyed the company of canines more. A deep connection to the creatures lived inside him. When he was younger, he would tell classmates he was a descendant of wolves. This resulted in kids making fun of him, but he didn't care. To him people represented disappointment and loneliness. Dogs gave the complete opposite.

After lacing his boots, Wyler climbed out of the Bronco. He did some light stretching while he took in the beauty of one of Lake Lanier's inlets. The sky was clear and the air carried scents of hickory and moss. Wyler released a short, sharp whistle. Moments later, Blackjack emerged from the woods, drawn back by the command. The two walked the lake perimeter for a mile before returning to the Bronco. They piled in and drove into the heart of Atlanta, where Wyler found a charging station.

With some time to kill, Wyler and Blackjack roamed the city until they stumbled on a diner. Wyler bought them egg sandwiches and hashbrowns. Forty-five minutes later, they returned to the Bronco and set off on the final leg of their trip. They arrived in Brewton, Alabama, a shade past two in the afternoon. It was Monday. Wyler parked in front of the animal hospital where Arlo said the drug-filled greyhound died.

"Ask for Hudson Benton," Arlo had said. "He'll help you with anything you need."

Wyler and Blackjack entered the hospital. Smells of fur and dander greeted them as they approached the receptionist.

"Hello," she said. "Do you have an appointment today?"

"No," Wyler said, smiling. "I'm looking for Hudson Benton. He should be expecting me."

"Hudson, ok, sure." She consulted her watch. "Right now, he should be out back." She rose and waved. "I'll bring you to him."

They followed her down a hallway and into a gated patch of grass measuring about twenty square yards. A man wearing dark gray medical scrubs guided an Australian cattle dog with a casted leg along the back fence.

The sight of the dog stopped Wyler in his tracks, taking him back to when he was eight years old, and his mother surprised him with a dog. An Australian cattle dog mixed with German Shepherd. At the time, Wyler didn't care that the dog was a bribe for forgiveness from years of parental neglect. He was immediately intrigued by the animal. Its coat was gray with patches of tan along his chest and neck. Symmetrical swaths of black fur coated the dog's ears, trailing down to create loops around his eyes. A white band of fur streaked down the center of its face. Wyler named him Patches—the brother he never had.

"Hudson," the receptionist called. "You've got a visitor."

Hudson waved at her in acknowledgment.

Turning to Wyler she said, "You two have a nice day."

"Thanks. You too," he said, walking into the yard.

As the receptionist left, she smiled more at Blackjack than Wyler.

The two men and two dogs met in the middle. The cattle dog hobbled excitedly over to Blackjack, sniffing every inch of him. Blackjack offered little in return for a greeting. Being leash-free allowed him to remain at a comfortable distance from the eager nose of the cattle dog. Wyler crouched, allowing the injured dog to sniff his hand. The dog wasted no time in allowing Wyler to pet him.

"Would you look at that," Hudson said.

"What?"

"This dog has been with us for two weeks now. The staff and the other dogs avoid him at all costs. Besides me, you're the first person that's been able to touch him."

Wyler shrugged, not surprised by the information. "I understand dogs better than I do people. They must sense it I guess."

"Anything's possible."

"I used to have a dog like this growing up," Wyler said. "Don't see too many of them around."

"They're a unique breed that's for sure. A good working dog. Lots of energy."

"I know it. We used to terrorize the seagulls along the beach where I grew up for hours. Felt like I could never tire that dog out."

Wyler stood, and offered his hand to Hudson. "My name's Ethan King." It was the first lie Wyler told the man, followed by the second. "I'm a contractor for the American Society for the Prevention of Cruelty to Animals. Someone should have reached out to you to let you know I was coming." Arlo kept Wyler's job title vague and tied the work to a large organization also in a vague way. If anyone questioned Wyler on his credentials, they were funneled to a close friend of Arlo's who held a high position in the organization and could back up Wyler's story. Arlo's contact never met Wyler and intentionally knew little about him. If something significant happened, the organization could easily disavow knowing Wyler, keeping Arlo insulated.

Hudson stood about an inch under Wyler's height of six feet. He had broad shoulders and dense forearms that fed into a solid core of someone who exercised regularly. From the streak of gray running through Hudson's unruly beard, Wyler placed the man's age in his late 40s or early 50s. Alert brown eyes stared out from a pair of thick-rimmed glasses framing a friendly face. Hudson accepted the outstretched hand with a smile.

"Yes, of course," Hudson said. "I've been waiting for you. You're here about that greyhound we brought in a week or so back, yeah?"

"That's right."

"Well, we appreciate the help and interest. Most people couldn't care less. The cops sure as hell didn't bat an eye. Par for the course, though. That poor dog looked like it had been through a lot. Malnourished, some lacerations on the haunches, plus the drugs. Tough way for her to go out."

"Have you seen anything like that before in a dog around here?"

"We get a steady supply of strays who have seen better days but not many greyhounds. And certainly not with that amount of drugs in their system. Sometimes we'll get people coming in when a dog gets into their pain meds after a surgery or something, but those are ninety-nine percent of the time accidents and not strays."

Wyler nodded. "I was told you can take me to where she was found?"

"I can, yeah. Let me get ol' Lemonade here settled, and then I can drive you out to the spot."

"Appreciate it," Wyler said. "And I've got kind of a weird request."

"Shoot."

"Do you happen to have an item the dog touched? A blanket, a collar, a toy, anything would help."

Hudson thought for a moment. "I'll check. I think we might still have the collar. Give me ten minutes. I'll meet you guys out front."

Wyler and Blackjack waited by the Bronco. From inside his jacket, Wyler produced a coin the size of a poker chip. He preferred the heavier weight compared to the standard chips. Starting at his thumb, he rolled the coin over the tops of his fingers until he reached his pinky, at which point, his thumb looped under and brought the coin back to the beginning. He repeated the movement, increasing the speed with each pass. A habit he developed anytime he had to wait. He preferred it to mindlessly scrolling his phone.

Hudson emerged from the hospital, having changed from his scrubs into jeans and a t-shirt.

"Ready?" Wyler said.

"Yes, sir. And I found this," Hudson said, handing Wyler a small Ziplock bag with a collar inside. "We took it off her first thing when she came in, so there shouldn't be anything else on it. Is that what you're looking for?"

"That'll do."

"I'm over there," Hudson said, pointing to a large black Dodge Ram. I can't stay with you guys, so if you plan to spend some time there, I recommend you follow me. Otherwise, I can give you a lift."

"I'll drive us. Lead the way."

Wyler trailed the Ram out of the parking lot. The truck led them through the town and into vast expanses of farmland offset by dense forests. After a fifteen-minute drive, Hudson pulled over to the side of a desolate road bordering a farm. The three of them regrouped in between the vehicles.

"That house there," Hudson said, motioning into the distance, "is where they found her."

"Is it mostly farms out here?"

"A decent amount. Go a little farther south into Florida, and it's a good patch of state forest."

"Will the farmer talk to me?"

"I don't see why not. Clyde's not a huge talker, but he's friendly enough. We can head up there, and I'll introduce you."

Wyler nodded. As they walked the driveway leading to the house, Wyler said, "Are drugs a problem around here?"

"I don't know, to be honest with you. I'm not in that kind of scene. I'd bet some people use, but in a small town like this, it's not in your face, at least. I'd imagine there's more in some of the cities. Mobile doesn't have the greatest reputation. A lot of rough areas there, where drugs would be a bigger issue."

"Makes sense."

Blackjack stopped abruptly, and peered to his left, focused on something. Wyler shielded his eyes from the sun as he studied the direction Blackjack's head aimed. A hundred yards off, a man hunched next to a wire fence.

"Is that him?" Wyler said.

Hudson scanned the horizon until he saw what they were looking at. He squinted, then said, "Yeah, that's him."

The man didn't react to their presence and kept on working. When Wyler, Blackjack, and Hudson reached him, he stood, leaning against a shovel.

"Clyde," Hudson said.

"Hudson."

"This is Ethan King. Ethan, this is Clyde Goyer."

"Ok," Clyde said, not moving to shake hands. The man examined him with an eye of suspicion.

"He had a few questions for you about the greyhound you found," Hudson said.

"You're here about a dog?" Clyde said. His eyebrows arched as he reexamined Wyler. "Why?"

"Mr. Goyer, I work for an organization that deals in cruelty to animals. And the dog you found seemed to fit the bill. I'm here to get some facts and see if this is an isolated incident."

"Really?" Clyde said. "Well, there's not much to tell. My daughter found the dog over by the treeline there. Must have come out of the woods."

"Anything like this ever happened before?" Wyler said.

"No."

"Are your neighbors missing a dog, or do they own greyhounds?"

"Beats me."

"Would you have a problem if we searched the woods?"

"Sure. My property ends about fifty yards past the treeline, so what you do out there doesn't make any difference to me. You might get onto other people's land. If you go far enough east, you'll hit the state forest. South, you'll cross into Florida. We're right on the border here."

"Ok," Wyler said. "I won't take any more of your time then. I'm going to grab some stuff from my ride, and we'll head in."

"Alright," Clyde said.

When they returned to the vehicles, Hudson said, "Are you guys all set with me?"

"For now, yeah," Wyler said. "If anything comes up, or I've got more questions for you, I'll give you a shout."

"Sounds good. The number your organization used to contact me is my cell."

"Thanks for the help, Hudson."

"Anytime. Good luck."

Hudson stepped up into his truck and drove off. Wyler tilted the driver seat forward in the Bronco and opened the floor storage. From inside, he pulled out the 35L tactical backpack. Out of habit, he unzipped the bag to do an inventory check. Satisfied everything he needed was still there, Wyler removed the water bottle and filled it from his jug. The kit was overkill, but going into an unknown area, especially a vast forest, he preferred to play it safe. He swung the backpack on, closed the storage door, then grabbed the dog collar before locking the Bronco.

Wyler and Blackjack cut through the farmer's land until they reached the rough location where the greyhound was discovered. Their demeanors changed, switching to a narrow-focused unit committed to completing a task. Wyler removed the collar from the bag, hoping enough of a scent remained in the fabric and the landscape for Blackjack to lock onto.

"Blackjack," Wyler said, waiting until his partner came to attention. Then he held the collar out for Blackjack to sniff. "Find it."

Blackjack's nose analyzed the collar, probing for the unique scents that would guide his path. After a few seconds, he transitioned from the collar to the ground, working his way methodically over the grass. Wyler trailed behind, watching the canine's body language for any indications he had found something. As they covered the terrain, Wyler periodically held out the collar for another sniff and repeated his command. Blackjack weaved back and forth. He stopped at certain areas for prolonged analysis before moving on. After twenty minutes of searching, Wyler questioned their odds of success. He recalled some experts giving the best guess scents lasted between five to fourteen days. From what Arlo had told him, they were still within that window of time. They pushed on, edging deeper into the woods. Then Blackjack stopped. His nose twitched at a particular hunk of matted grass. He studied the blades of grass and the dirt with great interest. Then he sat down. He'd found the scent.

"Dog on scent," Wyler said. "Now, find it."

Blackjack resumed his position and trotted into the woods. Wyler hung back ten yards, only advancing after Blackjack did. They moved together in a steady rhythm. Wyler estimated they traveled a little over a mile. About three-quarters of a mile farther, the wall of trees opened. They spilled out into a natural path of some kind. To Wyler's left, a quarter of a mile off, he detected another break in the treeline. Blackjack, however, turned right. As they continued, Wyler scanned the ground. A worn texture creased the grass as if it had been trampled. In one section of bare earth lay a patterned mark about the length of his foot. *A tire tread.* And twenty feet later, he found the imprint of a paw. They continued up a slight rise until they reached another clearing. It had the fingerprint of man on it. Stumps of trees were cut cleanly with symmetry to the space. Too orderly for nature.

Blackjack circled an area near the entrance, sniffing furiously. He circled again, then sat down, signaling the trail ended here.

"Good boy," Wyler said as he scratched Blackjack's head. Wyler took out his phone and opened a map app. He dropped a pin on his current location for future reference. "So, what the hell was a greyhound with a gut full of drugs doing out here?"

Straight ahead, another path led deeper into the woods. Wyler walked over to it. Two bare streaks of dirt sandwiched a strip of grass he determined was a road. A road meant people. And people meant possible clues left behind. Focused on the ground, Wyler made lawn mower passes back to where Blackjack stopped. He counted fifty steps before making each turn. Halfway through the slow plod, he caught a glimpse of something. He crouched and plucked a cigarette butt from a clump of dirt. Rolling the orange filter through his fingers, and based on the state of the remaining paper, he gauged it as a relatively fresh one. *So, potentially someone drove the dog out here. What was the goal? Were there multiple dogs, then? Some sort of exchange? And one of them got loose? Using greyhounds as drug mules? Suppose that's possible, but why here? Why this spot?*

Wyler pondered the questions as he finished his sweep. With no other clues, he called to Blackjack, who was exploring the perimeter.

"Blackjack. Let's go."

They retraced their steps to where they first came onto the path and continued past it until they reached a similar clearing. However, this one spanned a greater size and had three dirt roads branching off it. Tire tracks crisscrossed the land. Wyler checked his watch. Two hours had passed since they first set off.

"Ready for a break?"

Blackjack barked once. Wyler sat on a tree stump and filled the stainless steel cup for Blackjack to drink.

"What do you make of this?" Wyler said out loud, talking to Blackjack as if he were another human, and he might answer him with something other than a bark. While Wyler sipped from the bottle, he dropped another pin on his map, marking both clearings. He tucked away the phone, then grabbed a packet of jerky out of the backpack. He tossed two pieces to Blackjack and gnawed on one himself. His mind drifted as he ate the snack, playing out scenarios of what was happening behind the scenes with the dead greyhound.

A low growl shook him from the trance. Wyler glanced at Blackjack, who faced the opposite end of the clearing, hunched in an attack position.

"What do you have?" Wyler said, loading the items into the backpack while his eyes searched the vicinity for threats. As he stood, a stream of forceful air brushed past him. He flinched as something lodged into the tree next to him with a dull thump. A hunting arrow stuck out of the heart of a hickory half a foot from Wyler's head.

Chapter 6

Wyler dropped to a knee, staring at where the shot came from. As he opened his mouth to give a command to Blackjack, a voice shouted out.

"I wouldn't run if I was you."

A man holding a crossbow stepped from the treeline to their right. The man wore camouflage pants, a white t-shirt, and a black Crimson Tide hat. He was scrawny with a faint blonde goatee. Then another man strolled out from the left side, armed with the same weapon. He was taller and stouter than the first man, wearing jeans and a t-shirt with the sleeves cut away. A nest of black hair sat atop a head comparable to a watermelon. Straight ahead, where the arrow originated, emerged a third man. Medium height with greasy pilsner colored hair. A scar cut across both lips, stopping at the base of his chin. He pointed his empty crossbow toward the sky, sauntering forward with a cocky grin smeared across his broad face. The man scratched his chest above the worn graphic of a Judas Priest album.

"We've got a smart one, boys," Judas said. "He didn't run."

"This is private property," said Crimson Tide.

They closed within five feet of Wyler and Blackjack, each staying in their lanes, blocking them from an easy escape. Wyler assessed his situation as he would a game of Hold 'em. *Average hand. An unsuited jack nine or pocket eights, pre-flop. Crossbows instead of visible guns. One crossbow unloaded. The other two, once fired, would take time to reload. Guys are overconfident. Feel strong from their numbers and weapons.* All points Wyler planned to exploit. His final analysis led him to kick things off with a bluff.

"Sorry. I didn't know this was private property," Wyler said. "We were hiking. Guess we got a little turned around."

The men exchanged glances.

"He looks like a Fed to me," Crimson Tide said.

"Are you a Fed?" Judas said.

"No."

"He's got law written all over him," Crimson Tide said.

"Well, I could say what you look like, but it wouldn't be the greatest way to make friends," Wyler said.

Judas laughed. Shrill like a dying crow. "Shit, boys, not only is he smart, but he's funny too."

"Funny, my ass," Crimson Tide said. "Let's see how funny he thinks it is being stuck like a pig."

"I didn't mean anything by it," Wyler said. "We'll head out and see ourselves off of your land."

"You got any ID?" Judas said.

"What?"

"ID. Identification. Something to let us know you're not with the Feds."

"Why would you be worried about them?"

"Because we like the government to stay out of our business."

"And what business is that?"

"He's definitely a Fed," Crimson Tide said. "Listen to him asking these fucking questions."

"Just being friendly. If you move, we can be on our way."

"Something's off about this guy." Crimson Tide narrowed his eyes.

"How about that ID?" Judas said.

"Listen, unless you guys are cops I'm not giving you anything."

"Hiding something," Big Head chimed in. The other two men grinned at his contribution to the conversation. Wyler studied their faces and didn't like what they told him. *Flop turned up nothing. Change the strategy.* Wyler stepped back, clearing space for Blackjack to go right or left if needed.

"I like your dog," Judas said. "How much for him?"

"He's not for sale."

"Everything can be negotiated."

"Not for him, it can't."

Judas pulled his hat by the brim and wiped the sweat from his face with the back of his forearm, then he returned the hat. He grinned at Wyler.

"Well, if the mutt isn't for sale," Judas said. "I guess we can just take him."

"You're more than welcome to try," Wyler said, matching Judas's grin.

Wyler sensed the other men shifting their crossbows after the threat. *The river and the turn no help either. One advantage. Surprise. Go all in and see where the chips fall.*

Judas glanced at Crimson Tide, who acknowledged him by

lazily leveling his crossbow at Wyler's stomach. He slouched with an assurance Wyler wouldn't put up a fight.

"Blackjack," Wyler said. "You take three o'clock, and I've got nine. Good?"

Blackjack barked once.

Judas laughed, amused. "Shit, would you look at that. He's got him trained like a little circus dog."

The other two joined in on the laughter. *Keep laughing.* Wyler crept his right hand into his back pocket and slipped his fingers into the knuckleduster. Then, he said to Blackjack, "Go."

In one fluid motion, Wyler dove left, and Blackjack sprang to the right. Crimson Tide, startled by the dog lunging for him, stumbled back, raising his arms instinctively to shield himself from the attack. Blackjack leaped and bit down hard on Crimson Tide's wrist. A high-pitched scream bleated from his throat as the 195 pounds of pressure per square inch of jaws compressed against his flesh down to the bone. As Blackjack's body mass swung back to the ground, the momentum wrenched Crimson Tide forward. His other hand holding the crossbow swung wildly behind him and squeezed the trigger, sending his arrow careening harmlessly into the distance.

At the same instant, Wyler maneuvered into a crouched position on one knee in front of Big Head. Wyler cranked his arm back, then drove his fist with the knuckleduster into the inside of Big Head's knee. Big Head yelled out. "Son of a bitch." As his body crumpled to the earth, Wyler pressed forward like a sprinter off the line, slamming his shoulder into Big Head's chest, sending them toppling over. Wyler rolled forward over Big Head's face, spinning around smoothly on the grass, staying low. Quickly, he reached for the other knuckleduster.

Dazed, Big Head turned and raised the crossbow. Wyler bent his left arm and swung it under the weapon, forcing it toward the air. The bolt snapped, launching the arrow high. Not wasting a second, Wyler smashed his right fist into Big Head's stomach, then followed it up with a left-hand jab into his cheekbone. As Big Head fell backward, Wyler moved in closer, still on his knees. Wyler grabbed Big Head by the shirt with his left hand, stopping his descent. Then he yanked on the shirt pulling Big Head toward him. Wyler's right fist collided with the bridge of Big Head's nose, creating a crunching sound as metal decimated cartilage.

Wyler released the unconscious man, not waiting to see the body touch dirt. Instead, he pivoted and hopped to his feet, swiveling to find his next attacker. But none came. Amidst the flurry of violence, Judas struggled to successfully load and cock his crossbow. He paused as he locked eyes with Wyler, who hunched with his bloody fists swaying in front of him, ready to unleash further havoc. Crimson Tide's screams drew Judas's focus next. The blood drained from his face as his cohort flailed and hissed at the dog thrashing his damaged arm. The fight or flight mechanism filled Judas's eyes.

He decided on flight.

Judas let the crossbow tumble from his hands. Then he took off for the farthest tree line.

"Release." Wyler shouted to Blackjack. The dog twisted one last time before dropping the arm. Then Wyler said, "Get." He pointed to Judas. Blackjack scanned the horizon until he zeroed in on the fleeing man. His paws kicked up dirt as he sprinted after his prey. Wyler walked over to Crimson Tide, who rocked back and forth, clutching his wrist in pure agony.

"My...my hand...I can't feel my fucking hand," Crimson Tide said.

"And now you're not going to feel your face."

Crimson Tide turned his head just as the heel of Wyler's boot smashed into his forehead. The impact flattened Crimson Tide on his back. Wyler stepped to the side and then kicked Crimson Tide in the temple until the lights went off behind his eyes. With two of the attackers subdued, Wyler checked the progress of Blackjack.

Judas got to within ten yards of the treeline when Blackjack caught him. Like Crimson Tide, the dog clamped onto an arm and dragged the man down. The scream of terror rippled through the air. Wyler jogged the thirty yards to join the action. As he got closer, Judas grappled for something in his pocket. When his hand cleared the fabric, Judas flipped his wrist. And like a magic trick a knife suddenly appeared.

Wyler broke into a flat-out run. He slid like a quarterback giving himself up, extending his arm as a shield between the blade and Blackjack. The knife landed on the meat of Wyler's forearm. Judas dragged the knife, slicing through the flesh. Despite the pain, Wyler caught the retreating wrist as he rose to his knees. With his free hand, Wyler drove home a right-handed hook that crashed into Judas's ear. The concussion forced him to drop the knife. Wyler stood, keeping hold of the wrist, while Blackjack pinned the other. Wyler thrust Judas's arm behind his back. Once he had it secured, Wyler put Judas in a choke hold with his right arm, squeezing with all his force until the man blacked out.

Panting, Wyler relaxed his muscles and backed away from the limp body.

"Release," Wyler said to Blackjack. The arm fell from Blackjack's mouth like a dead pheasant. "Good boy." Wyler surveyed the area. All three assailants remained immobile on the ground. As the adrenaline faded, the gash on Wyler's arm throbbed.

"Blackjack. Backpack. Go."

The dog turned and trotted across the field. While Wyler waited, he rummaged through Judas's pockets. Out of them, he produced a wallet, lighter, phone, chewing tobacco, a small yellow envelope, and a dozen keys on a chain. Sitting on the ground, Wyler opened the wallet first. It contained sixty dollars cash and three credit cards. The driver's license said his name was Sidney Rut. An unflattering name Wyler thought fit the unconscious man at his feet. He pictured people calling the man Sid. After the wallet, Wyler opened the envelope, which held six circular white pills. Wyler picked one out and stuck it in his own pocket.

Then Sid's phone pinged. On the screen a notification read, *Motion Detected*. Curious, Wyler swiped the notification, and an app opened. A live video feed appeared. Trotting across the frame was Blackjack with the backpack clenched in his mouth. Wyler looked up from the screen to see his canine partner approaching.

Cameras? He exited the full-screen footage, which put him into the menu screen for the app. Six thumbnails populated the page, each representing a different camera. He tapped through them and found they covered the entire field. A gut instinct made Wyler take out his phone and snap a photo of the account profile of the app. Once he gleaned whatever information he could from the items, Wyler meticulously returned them to Sid's pockets. If these guys were involved with the dead greyhound, he wanted them to carry on as usual. He wanted them to think the beatings were an act of self-defense and nothing more.

Blackjack set the backpack at Wyler's feet. He paced by his side, nudged the wounded arm, and licked the skin.

"I'm alright," Wyler said, petting Blackjack on the head.

From the backpack, Wyler grabbed the first aid kit. The cut

spanned roughly three inches. It didn't appear too deep. He washed the wound with water, then doused it with hydrogen peroxide. With two large Band-Aids, he covered the cut. Then he wrapped gauze over his forearm for added protection.

Sid moaned then, and his fingers twitched. Wyler loaded the backpack and got to his feet.

"Let's go," he said to Blackjack.

They hustled off, disappearing moments later into the woods, leaving behind their trail of human wreckage.

Chapter 7

Wyler and Blackjack stepped on the road outside Clyde's farm as the sun dipped closer to the horizon. They found the Bronco a few yards down right where they'd left it. Wyler harnessed Blackjack in his seat, then typed in the address for the nearest hotel on his phone. He wanted a shower, and a hotel was the easiest way to get one, despite his preference to sleep in the Bronco. A Best Western came up. He turned on the engine, and they were off. Along the way, they picked up food, a steak and cheese grinder for Wyler and a grilled chicken sandwich with sweet potato fries for Blackjack. Thirty minutes later, they pulled into the hotel lot, finding a spot nestled in the rear of the building.

"Wait here," Wyler said. Blackjack snorted in disapproval. "Don't give me that. I want to make sure this place will allow a brute like you in here first." Blackjack snorted again, then turned his back to Wyler. "I'll chalk the attitude up to you having a long day."

As he walked to the entrance, Wyler threw on his jacket to cover the wound on his arm. After providing the concierge with his fake ID, he paid cash, then returned to the SUV. He opened the passenger door and unhooked Blackjack's harness.

"We've got the green light. Let's go, your majesty."

Inside the room, Wyler cranked the air conditioning as low as it would go, then filled Blackjack's bowl with water. They ate their meals together, sitting on the floor. When they finished, Wyler attended to Blackjack.

"Are you ready?"

Blackjack barked once.

Wyler worked his fingers through the thick fur, feeling for any ticks or cuts. Finding none, he checked the nails on each paw, filing away any cracked or split pieces. With the flashlight of his phone, Wyler inspected the inside of Blackjack's ears, then his eyes for abnormalities. When that task was complete, Wyler applied a healthy scoop of dog toothpaste to a brush and cleaned Blackjack's teeth. This particular habit had taken Wyler the longest to master with his furry brethren. They had sparred for a good six months until Blackjack finally relented. Blackjack drank some water to clear the toothpaste from his mouth as Wyler took out a brush.

"You did good today. You brought fear to those boys. Remember that feeling," Wyler said as he ran the bristles through the tan coat. This part of their nightly routine they enjoyed the most. It served as a meditative decompression from whatever events the day held. Wyler focused on quadrants of the dog's body, removing clumps of fur with each pass. The process took under thirty minutes. Wyler scratched Blackjack's chest, then packed away the grooming supplies.

"All set," he said. "I'm going to clean up. Get some rest."

Blackjack hopped onto the bed, circled a corner, then settled into position with a sigh. In the bathroom, Wyler removed the gauze and Band-Aids from his forearm. The wound was raw but didn't show signs of infection. He stripped naked and showered. After toweling dry, he applied fresh bandages and then dressed in clean jeans and a t-shirt. He fixed himself a weak coffee from the machine in the room. As he took his first sip, he considered the day's events and what he'd learned.

Two connected clearings, both showing signs of recent human activity. The path between them was too narrow for a truck to drive through, but there were possible indicators of a smaller vehicle. Blackjack confirmed the greyhound had been there at some point. Wyler opened his map app and studied the surrounding area of the marking pins he'd dropped. Few houses existed within a ten-mile radius. *Someone brought the dog there from another location. Who dropped the dog off? Were the guys in the second clearing involved? Why crossbows? And why the cameras? Hunters? Six cameras, though? Why that many? Was that how they knew he was there in the clearing? They thought he was with law enforcement. Would they have thought that if they were just farmers hunting their land? Would they have come at him with so much aggression otherwise?* He found it unlikely.

Wyler rooted the pill he'd taken from Sid out of his jeans on the floor. *Would this pill match the one the hospital found in the greyhound's stomach?* Wyler texted Hudson a message, asking if there were pictures of the pills extracted from the dog. A picture of one wouldn't prove anything, but it could help him see if getting the pill tested would be worth it. The working theory Wyler landed on was someone from side A had access to one or potentially more greyhounds. They stuffed them with drugs, brought them

to the clearing, and sent them to side B, where presumably someone removed the drugs to sell. Why that particular location,
he couldn't say yet. Arlo wanted to know if this was a single or
recurring incident. At the moment, Wyler leaned toward there
being something bigger going on, but he'd need more proof. And
he knew someone who might be able to help.

Wyler stepped out of the convenience store forty-five minutes
later. He pried open the plastic shell of the burner smartphone
he'd purchased. Sitting in the front seat of the Bronco, Wyler
probed his memory for the number he was sworn to memorize
and to never write down or store. He punched the number in
and waited. After a few clicks and pockets of dead air, a voice
answered.

"Hello. What is your access code, please?"

"Delta Echo Charlie. Whiskey India Lima," Wyler said.

"And your number?"

"6-14-88."

The line clicked and went silent. Then another familiar voice
answered.

"Declan, how the hell are you?"

"I'm good, Jon. How's business treating you?"

"Well, I'm still alive, and there's still plenty of secrets to hear
and trade."

Wyler met Jon Mack during his third tour in Afghanistan.
Mack at the time worked for the CIA. After a disagreement over
an assignment, Mack left the agency and went out on his own,
helping those with similar ideals and more importantly, deep
pockets.

"What do you need?" Mack asked.

"I need login access to an app without the account holder knowing I'm in there."

"I see. And this someone is on the wrong side of the law?"

"More than likely."

"Foreign or domestic?"

"Domestic. And this is the information I have," Wyler said, then read the camera app details from the photo he'd taken of Sid's phone.

"Ok," Mack said. "And when do you need this by?"

"The sooner the better."

"Can get it to you in a few hours if you want, but that'll come with a heftier price tag."

"That's fine."

Mack laughed. "He doesn't even ask how much heftier. So, you're doing someone else's bidding again?"

"Just helping out a friend."

"Same friend as last time?"

"Yeah."

"Ok. Nothing wrong with that. I'll get him the invoice through the same back channels. Once it's paid, I'll get somebody on it. Shouldn't be too hard of a job."

"I appreciate it."

"In the meantime, download the app onto your personal phone. I'll text you back on this number with instructions once we've got access."

"Got it. I'm not sure where this operation will take me, so I might need you again in a few days."

"As promptly and as exorbitantly as you two pay, I'll be here."

Wyler grinned. "Thanks."

"Any time. Keep an eye on your six," Mack said, then hung up.

Wyler slipped the phone into his pocket and headed back to the hotel. Blackjack cracked open one eye, confirmed who had come in, then returned to his slumber. Wyler set the phone on the dresser, then habitually tapped his pockets. From the back two, he removed the knuckledusters. Flecks of red coated the titanium. He took them to the bathroom sink, and rinsed the blood off. Using a washcloth, he dried the metal, then placed them on the nightstand, ready to go for whatever came next.

Chapter 8

Jed burst from the truck before the tires finished their last rotation. He ran to the rear of the trailer, fumbling to unlatch his belt. Clayton killed the ignition and climbed out. The four-hour drive strained his lower back and made his knees feel swollen. And the severe case of swamp ass he suffered didn't help matters either. He walked to where Jed had disappeared to find him pissing in the dirt.

"For Christ's sake," Clayton said, shielding his eyes. "Would you put your goddamn dick away and act like an adult."

"When nature calls, I answer her."

"You couldn't have gone inside?"

"It was past the point of no return. If I had to take one more step, I would have pissed my pants. Is that what you would've preferred?"

"I would've preferred it if you were born with a few more brain cells."

Jed laughed as he zipped his pants. "I've got more than enough, thank you."

"Come on. I don't want to be here all afternoon."

They stepped onto the porch of the main house on the sprawling twenty-acre farm. Clayton knocked on the front door. A few seconds later, a gray-haired man opened it.

"Hi ya, Clayton. Jed," the man said. He wore a baggy short-sleeve plaid button down and jeans. A pair of suspenders hung by his sides.

"Hi, Burt," Clayton said. He hardly recognized the man in front of him. It had only been three years since Clayton had seen Burt Hereford, but the state of his body made it seem closer to fifteen. Time had not been kind to the man.

"Jesus, Burt. What the hell happened to you?"

"Goddamn heart attack, that's what."

"When did that happen?"

"Last summer. All the stress. Finally got to me, I guess. If the wife wasn't home, I'd be a goner for sure. These liberal pussies and these damn hippie organizations and all their laws. They turned everyone against us and ruined the whole industry. Florida used to be the mecca for dog racing. Now, what do we got?"

A woman's voice called from deeper in the house. "Burt, don't get heated again."

"I'm fine," he shouted back. He grumbled under his breath to Clayton. "She's always on my ass now. It's worse than the damn heart attack was."

"That's women," Clayton said.

"Tell me about it," Burt said. "Let me get my boots on, and we can head over."

In a small nook next to the door, Burt pulled on a pair of shin-high rubber boots. The three men walked sixty yards to a massive red barn. A farm hand hustled to Burt's side and assisted him in opening the large double doors. A rank smell of rotting meat swept over the men as the stale air exited the barn. Along the left wall, running the length of it, rested two rows of cages, fifty total. An assortment of tables, lights, and breeding equipment occupied the center space. The right-hand wall housed three industrial-sized refrigerators and stacks of dried dog food.

"Take a look around," Burt said. "I've got thirty dogs you can take. Five of them aren't worth a damn and are scheduled for meeting their maker if you know what I mean."

They sauntered down the aisle of cages, which were barely big enough for the dogs inside to comfortably stand.

"I was surprised to get your call," Burt said. "Your track closed, didn't it? All us breeders now got a ton of inventory with no buyers. I heard Ray, you remember him? Ran the Calypso track?"

"Yeah, I remember Ray."

"I don't know if I believe it, but I heard instead of turning his hounds over to shelter groups, as a fuck you to them, he fed the dogs to his alligators."

"No way," Jed said.

"That's what I heard anyway. He supposedly did it for a week straight. Had people come out and bet on which dog got eaten first and by which gator."

"Ray was always a bit off," Clayton said. "I wouldn't put it past him."

"True enough," Burt said. "So what do you have planned for them? You got an inside line on something I don't know about?"

"Nothing you need to concern yourself with."

"Is that right?" Burt pulled out a handkerchief and wiped the sweat from his forehead, then his upper lip. "You can trust me. Your father did anyway."

"Well, he's not around anymore, is he?"

"I was sorry to hear about his passing," Burt said. "Is it true he shot himself?"

Agitation rose through Clayton's chest. He snapped at Burt. "Yeah. He stuck the barrel right in his mouth and pulled the trigger. Can we move this along?"

Burt stared at Clayton for a long moment, then spit on the ground and shuffled forward. "Alright. How many you want?"

"I'll take all of them."

"All of them, huh?" Burt said, raising an eyebrow.

"Is that a problem?"

Burt ignored the question and instead got the attention of the farmhand. "Hey, go with Jed, and show him where to park their truck."

The farmhand nodded and walked out of the barn with Jed. Once they were gone, Burt focused on Clayton. The sincerity vanished from his face.

"Now, about the price..." Burt said.

"What about it?" Clayton said, stepping closer to Burt. "You said two hundred per dog on the phone."

"Well, thinking about it some more, I think they're actually five hundred a dog."

"Are you fucking with me right now? I'm doing you a favor by taking these dogs off your hands. Frankly, you're lucky I was even going to give you two hundred for each."

Burt shrugged. "I think you're holding out on me, Clayton. I don't know what you're doing with these dogs, but you're doing something. And if you don't want to cut me in, fine, but then it will cost you more."

"I'm not doing anything you want in on. Trust me."

"Tell me what it is then."

"I'm not paying five hundred dollars a dog."

"I'm sorry to hear that," Burt said. He stared at his fingers and picked at a hangnail. "You can go find someone else then. I'd rather drown these dogs than give them away for nothing."

Clayton shook his head and rubbed a spot on his forehead where he felt a migraine developing. He glared at Burt. "I don't have that much to spend. Are you going to honor the deal you gave me on the phone? Or..."

"Or? Or what, Clayton? Was there a threat on the other end of that sentence?"

The agitation was transitioning into a rage. Clayton's heart quickened as he stared at the dogs. They were his lifeline to getting out of the mess he found himself in. *And like those mob pricks, here's another one trying to shake me down.*

"Two hundred dollars. Six grand. That's everything I've got."

"Not gonna do it," Burt said with a shrug. "You know, your father..."

Clayton spun and backhanded Burt across the face before he could finish the sentence. Caught off guard, Burt tumbled into a table, sending supplies crashing to the ground.

"Gah, damn," Burt said, massaging his cheek.

Clayton, a little surprised himself, grinned. Something else stirred inside him then. Empowerment. He felt good doling out some pain for a change instead of always being on the receiving end. His grin widened as he walked toward Burt.

"Now, Clayton...think about what you're doing," Burt stammered upon seeing the flames of hate stoked to life in Clayton's eyes. "I'll forgive the lapse in judgment, but..."

Clayton backhanded Burt again, this time across the other cheek. Burt moaned as he tripped and fell to the floor.

"You slimy son of a bitch," Clayton said. "Trying to take advantage of me, huh? You little cocksucker. Does that make you feel good?"

"Clayton, I was just..."

"You were just nothing," Clayton shouted, grabbing Burt by the ankle, preventing him from crawling away.

"Please," Burt said.

Clayton rolled Burt onto his back and punched him in the face. Each strike fed the monster of resentment starving inside Clayton. He hit him again, this time splitting Burt's lower lip. Blood seeped down his chin. The monster had a taste and wanted more. Clayton picked Burt up by the shoulders and dragged him toward a large open bin of dog food. The caged dogs barked and dug at the bars of their prisons as the men passed.

"You want to know what I'm doing so badly?" Claytond said. "Well, this is what it fucking feels like for what I'm dealing with."

Clayton shoved Burt's head into the bin of dog food.

"It feels like this, Burt. Like I'm fucking suffocating."

Burt's arms clawed at the air, clawed at Clayton's arm that deprived him of oxygen. When Burt's body slowed down, Clayton ripped him out of the bin, flinging bits of food across the barn. Burt gasped as Clayton slammed him against a support beam. Clayton kneed the man in the stomach for good measure. Burt coughed and wheezed. Bits of dog food spilled from his mouth.

"Now," Clayton said. "You're going to sell me these fucking dogs with no more questions asked. And what's that?" Clayton leaned his ear close to Burt's, pretending like he was telling him a secret. "You're going to give me a deal? Fifty dollars a dog. My god that is awfully generous of you."

Clayton released Burt, who slumped to the ground, still coughing and spitting. Out of his front pants pocket, Clayton removed an envelope of cash. He counted fifteen hundred dollars. Burt flinched as Clayton crouched next to him. Clayton shoved the money into Burt's shirt pocket.

"There we go," Clayton said, patting the pocket. "A done deal. And let me be clear. If you think of talking to anyone about this, someone like the boys in blue, I'll tell them about all of your little side operations and hustles. You know the ones I'm talking about. And we'll see who they take a greater interest in. Nod if you understand me?"

Burt hesitated. His eyes wide with fear and scorn. He spit a clumped wad of blood onto the floor, and then he nodded.

"Good. I'm glad that's settled."

Clayton hoisted Burt to his feet.

"Everything alright?" Jed said, coming into the barn. He and the farmhand stared at Burt and Clayton, then exchanged looks of their own.

"Burt here took a little spill. Tripped over something on the floor. He's ok," Clayton said. "Aren't you, Burt?"

"Yeah...yeah, that's right," Burt said.

The farmhand shifted nervously, but didn't speak up.

"Uh, ok," Jed said. "Can we start loading the dogs then?"

"Hell, yes," Clayton said with a phony lighthearted enthusiasm. "I already paid up, too. Let's get them in there."

"How many?"

"All thirty of them."

The farmhand sought Burt's approval. Burt waved a hand at

him to help. Clayton stuck close to Burt's side while Jed and the farmhand loaded the greyhounds into their trailer. Half an hour later, Jed said, "That's all of them."

"Alright, well, we'll get out of your hair then," Clayton said, slapping his hand hard on Burt's shoulder. "Give my love to the Mrs."

"Fuck you, Clayton," Burt said in a low growl under his breath.

"That's the spirit." Clayton grinned as he headed for the Chevy.

Once the truck doors closed, Jed turned to Clayton and said, "What the fuck happened in there?"

Still grinning, Clayton said, "I negotiated down the price."

"You did? How much?"

"Fifty a dog."

"Fifty," Jed said in shock. Then he hooted. "Hoo baby, you're good, Clayton."

"Good? You're goddamn right I am."

Two hours into the second leg of their journey, Jed took over driving. Clayton folded a worn sweatshirt into a pillow and tossed and turned until he found a halfway comfortable position.

"Wake me when we're fifteen minutes out," Clayton said.

"Ok, cuz," Jed said, throwing him a sardonic salute.

Within minutes, Clayton fell asleep. Dreams of faceless people and grotesquely shaped animals revisited him. He stood alone in the dark. Growls thick with blood in the throat surrounded him. As if some incomprehensible creature was feeding on corpses. The growls increased, and he ran, but he couldn't see through the darkness. The floor parted, and he fell for what felt like miles. He landed in a sticky, warm substance, immobilizing him. Something inside the liquid moved. It slithered over his body until it located his mouth and crawled in, devouring him from the inside out.

A hand touched him, and he jerked awake.

"Christ, Clayton," Jed said. "Are you alright? You were screaming."

"I was?"

"Yeah. I almost drove off the fucking road. You scared the shit out of me."

Clayton grunted. "What time is it?"

"Ten past nine. Maybe another hour to the spot."

"Nine? I slept that long? Felt like I was out for five minutes."

"Yeah," Jed said. He glanced at his cousin. "What were you dreaming about?"

"Shit, I don't know. Not sure how to even describe it."

"You know what I dream about? I dream about that big son of a bitch who cut my ear. I dream of how I'm going to kill the bastard as soon as I get the chance."

"Oh, yeah," Clayton said, sitting up in his seat. "How would you do it?"

"I'd take my Louisville slugger and bash his brains out. I bet that big stupid head of his would burst like a tractor-trailer running over a squirrel."

Clayton smirked. "Then what would you do with the body?"

"I'd leave it in the street for everyone to see what happens when you fuck with me."

"Don't you think they'd come to kill you after? If you left him for his friends to find."

"Well, maybe I'd bring him to Ray and let his gators make him disappear."

"Sounds like you've got more planning to do."

"That fucking prick."

Jed signaled and exited the highway. He navigated the streets

until they turned off onto back roads. They drove for another
thirty minutes until they arrived at their destination in a thick
mangrove. Jed flipped off the headlights as he approached a
barrier made out of the surrounding fauna. A moment later,
something tapped on Jed's window. He turned and then jumped
in his seat at the appearance of a man dressed in black, wearing
night vision goggles and carrying a pump action shotgun.

"Christ," Jed mumbled as he rolled down his window.

"What are you doing here?" the man said with a heavy accent.

"We're with Enzo Crippa. We're here for our pickup," Clayton
said across Jed.

The man stared at the two of them. He pressed near his ear
and spoke in Spanish. After he received a response, he said to Jed,
"Ok. Go through." Two other men seeped out of the foliage and
moved aside the barrier. When Jed looked out his window again,
the man had vanished. Jed eased the truck forward, pulling up to
a tin-roofed hut situated along a bank of a body of water. Another
man, dressed less paramilitary than the other, stepped up to the
driver's side. Jed opened the door, but the man pressed it closed.

"Stay in the truck," he said. "Where are the dogs?"

"In the trailer," Jed said, nodding behind him.

"How many?"

"There's thirty back there," Clayton said, leaning toward the
window.

"Ten need to be loaded now, si?"

"That's right. We've got a can of spray paint back there so you
can mark the dogs you load with the stuff."

The man stared at Clayton. Then he said, "Ok. Don't get out.
We'll let you know when it's done."

"Alright," Clayton said.

In the distance, out on the water, a red light flashed twice, then stayed on for a brief time longer, then turned off. The hum of an electric boat motor trickled into the truck cabin. Faint moonlight illuminated the outlines of four men on a small dingy. They pulled up to a dock along the edge of the hut. Three more men greeted the people on the boat. The packages were quickly transferred from the craft into the hut. After they offloaded the vessel, it drifted back from where it had come.

A half an hour passed before someone came out of the hut. It was yet another new man.

"Where are the dogs?" he said in a similar accent.

"I already told Jesus over there, they're in the trailer," Jed said.

"Jed," Clayton said, cutting off his cousin before he escalated the situation.

The man stared at Clayton and then at Jed as if debating slitting their throats.

"Ten," the man finally said.

"Ten dogs, that's right. Make sure you mark them."

The man retreated to the hut, shouting something in Spanish. Four men followed him out the door, two of which carried jam-packed pouches, while one held a feeding tube. The trailer door opened with a clang and the dogs yipped at the sight of the newcomers. More shouts came, followed by bursts of scuffling. Some of the dogs must have been fighting back against the tube being shoved down their throats. Clayton took a small satisfaction in their torment. Another half an hour passed. Then the trailer door slammed shut.

"You're all set," one of the men said at Jed's window.

"That's it?" Jed said. But the man had already turned away, heading for the hut. "Real friendly mother fuckers, aren't they?"

"Turn around up there, and let's get out of here while we can," Clayton said.

Jed did as he was told and spun the truck. They waited as the barrier was moved again. Jed accelerated through, and they were clear. Clayton held his breath until they were safely back on the highway. He checked the side view mirrors, looking for signs of someone following them. He peered into the night sky for any helicopters filled with DEA agents. But nothing stood out. Relieved, Clayton finally released his breath.

Chapter 9

Wyler and Blackjack rose early the next morning before the everyday hustle and bustle of people shipping off to work kicked into full effect. They walked for two miles, stopping at an empty park, where they jogged two more miles around a track. As they made their way back to the hotel, they ducked into a local diner. Wyler ordered their usual breakfast sandwiches, and they ate at a small metal table out front. The burner phone pinged while Wyler drank his coffee. A message from Mack showed on the screen. It provided Wyler with an access email and password to log in to Sid's security camera app. Another message followed reading, *If there are any issues, let me know. Otherwise, this concludes our service.* Wyler opened the app he'd installed on his phone the night before and entered the credentials. The loading icon spun. Then the identical homepage Wyler had seen on Sid's phone appeared. Wyler tapped on one of the camera thumbnails, and a live video feed of the field came into focus.

"He came through for us," Wyler said to Blackjack.

A few taps and scrolls later, Wyler enabled notifications for any movement in the field.

"Now, we wait."

Once he finished his coffee, Wyler took a photo of the login credentials with his phone, then deleted the messages. He scanned the vicinity for anyone looking at him. When no one was paying him any mind, he removed the SIM card from the burner phone. Using a napkin from his breakfast, he wiped the phone of any prints, then tossed the pieces into a trash can.

They returned to the hotel at ten. Wyler showered, then rebandaged his forearm. The wound didn't show signs of infection, which he was grateful for. It was sore, but the pain was tolerable. After getting dressed, Wyler tucked his knuckledusters into his back pockets. From the nightstand drawer, he found the pill he lifted from Sid, wrapped it in a tissue for protection, and placed it in the front pocket of his pants. Wyler tidied the room. Some habits from the military, he found, never died. As they exited the room, Wyler hung the *No Housekeeping Needed* sign on the door handle.

They climbed in the Bronco and drove to the animal hospital. The receptionist led them to Hudson's office.

"Hello, there," Hudson said, standing from his desk to extend his hand to Wyler.

"Thanks for seeing us again," Wyler said as he shook Hudson's hand.

"Don't mention it." He selected a folder from his desk and slid it to Wyler. "Here's the report on the greyhound we found. The photos of the pills are on the third page."

Wyler flipped through until he landed on the pictures he

wanted. He took Sid's pill from his pocket and studied it next to the photos.

"I'm not an expert," Wyler said. "But they look the same anyway. Did you have the other thing I asked for?"

"I do." Hudson walked to a leather satchel hanging behind the door and removed a wrapped object about the size of a popsicle. "An FTS, better known as a fentanyl test kit." As Hudson unwrapped the test, he said, "Do I want to know where you got that pill from?"

"Probably not."

Hudson frowned. "Do I need to worry about the cops coming to talk to me about you?"

"I doubt it. But if anything comes up, or someone approaches you, let me know. I'll handle it."

Hudson sighed as he grabbed a small beaker from a shelf. He picked up Wyler's pill, and using a pocket knife, he cut it in half. He dropped one portion of the pill into the beaker and broke it up with the knife point. Then he poured water into the beaker from a bottle on his desk, and stirred it with the knife. The test itself was a thin strip of paper. Hudson dipped the end of the test with wavy blue lines into the mixture. After fifteen seconds, he removed the test and laid it on a bare section of his desk.

"Ok," Hudson said. "It should be ready in five minutes at the most."

While they waited, Wyler sat in a chair opposite Hudson's desk. Hudson dropped back into his seat. He pointed at the bandage on Wyler's forearm.

"That's new since I saw you last. Did you get that at the same place you got this pill?"

Wyler shrugged. "You sound like a cop yourself."

"Sorry. I don't mean to pry. I know a lot of people who love dogs and would go to great lengths to help them, but if they thought there was some sort of criminal element involved...I don't know... I'm not sure many of them would be as interested as you seem to personally be."

"You'd be surprised."

"Would I?"

"Dogs operate with a simple outlook of love and loyalty, and friendship. If they bond with you, they give you all of themselves. And that's rare to find. So to me, they deserve the same respect and protection as we do. And for those who don't share in that respect, yeah, as you put it, I take it personally."

"Well put," Hudson said. He nodded at Blackjack. "And what about this guy? What's his story?"

Wyler glanced at Blackjack, then at Hudson. "I rescued him from a bad situation about four years ago. He was one of the lucky ones in a litter I found. He hasn't left my side since."

"He doesn't seem like he has your standard home pet kind of training."

Wyler grinned. "That's because he's not a pet. I taught him the majority of what he knows."

"Where did you learn that type of training?"

"Marines. I was a dog handler."

"No shit."

"No shit."

"Impressive," Hudson said. "I love being around dogs, but I don't have the patience for that level of training."

"I can't take all the credit," Wyler said, shifting slightly in his chair. "My ex...helped with some advanced skills. The stuff she knows and tests is light years beyond what anyone currently thinks dogs are capable of. What I can do is impressive. But what she can do is brilliant."

"Ex, huh?"

Wyler chuckled and sat up in his chair. "A story for another time. How are we looking on the test?"

Hudson leaned over the strip of paper, analyzing the results. "One pink line," he said as he referenced the paper for what that meant. "It's positive for fentanyl."

"You sure?"

"Yeah, these tests are pretty accurate."

"Ok."

"So what's that mean?"

"I'm not sure yet." He rose from the chair and turned for the door. "Thanks again for the help."

"I'll be here if anything else comes up."

Outside, Wyler and Blackjack got in the Bronco. Wyler drove with no destination in mind. He let his mind wander over the puzzle, figuring out what to do next. Something about what Sid had said to him floated through his thoughts. He had said they were on private property. As Wyler passed a scenic stretch of landscape, he pulled over, and they got out. While Blackjack sniffed the diverse smells of the area, Wyler used his phone to search Sid's name for a criminal record. Within a few minutes, he got a hit. Sydney Rut was arrested on a minor drug charge as a teenager, as well as an assault charge, which was dropped, and a more serious drug charge which he was convicted of and did three years in jail when he was in his twenties. Wyler closed the browser and opened his map to study the location pins he'd dropped yesterday. He panned over the area spotting three viable options for the property Sid referred to. From there, Wyler searched public records and real estate sites until he tracked the addresses of the homes. After a few more minutes, he had the registered names of the owners. They were Eugene Manning, Gus Fremont, and Mason Klempt.

He started with Eugene Manning. Wyler plugged in the name and searched the top social media sites. What he was hoping to find, he didn't really know. He was taking a shot in the dark to find a connection somewhere in the ether that would give him another avenue to explore. Twenty minutes later, he ruled Eugene Manning out. The man was an old farmer who loved Jesus, his family, and college football. Nothing to suggest he was involved with drug traffickers.

Gus Fremont turned up more of the same. Another ordinary person with an ordinary life and no clear signs they were involved. Having stared at his screen for over an hour, Wyler hopped off the open back of the Bronco where he'd been sitting. He rubbed the haze from his eyes and stretched his arms. Blackjack returned from his exploration of the area. He jumped into the Bronco. Wyler scratched him behind his ear and then filled his water bowl.

"I've got one more name to check. Then we can get out of here."

Wyler sat back down, and Blackjack took a seat next to him.

"Mason Klempt," Wyler said as he typed the name into the search engine. He scrolled briefly through the results and stopped on a link from a local news outlet with the title 'Local man with suspected ties to organized crime, questioned in the disappearance of...'

Wyler tapped the link, and the full article appeared. He read the opening paragraph.

'Alabama native Mason Klempt was brought in today for questioning by authorities regarding the disappearance of the up-and-coming political candidate for state office, Michael Berg.

Klempt, a man with suspected ties to organized crime operating out of Mobile, has declined any comments aside from stating his innocence. Michael Berg was running for local office under a Democratic platform and was the clear front runner until he disappeared two months before the elections.'

Wyler paused and then read through the remainder of the article. His heart rate increased as he hit the penultimate paragraph. He read a quote from Klempt's sister proclaiming police harassment. The sister's name, which the reporter wrote in its entirety, was Bethany Rut. *Sid's mother.* Wyler considered it too much of a coincidence to deny Sydney Rut was the nephew of Mason Klempt. *The drugs, the dogs, the locations, the family ties, crime history...has to be connected.* Nothing was proven, and he still didn't know much about where the dog originally came from. But the information provided him a new lead to explore.

In the satellite view on his map, Wyler zoomed in tight to the property of Mason Klempt. A cluster of four structures sat in the northeast quadrant of where Wyler roughed out their property line to stretch. One of the structures was a house. Another looked like a barn. He zoomed in tighter on the map, noting the roads leading in. The map pixelated the more he zoomed. A primary paved road led to the house and potentially two dirt roads. Wyler traced the dirt roads to where they connected with the main route outside their property. At the entrance of each, he dropped a marking pin. If he explored one of the buildings, the barn, maybe, he might confirm or rule out a connection. Again, he didn't know what he expected to find there, but he didn't have any better options other than to wait and see if the cameras turned up anything. On the map, he plotted a course for sneaking onto their land. They would go at night under cover of darkness.

Sid Rut sat on the second step of his Uncle's porch. He dug a fingernail amongst the five crude stitches in his left forearm, scratching an itch. *Fucking dog.* From his pocket he produced his stash of drugs. He tossed one of the fentanyl laced pills into his mouth and washed it down with the warm beer by his side. The stitches agitated him as much as the memory of the dog biting him—getting the better of him. *Fucking dog. Kill that fucker.* He sipped more beer. The drugs and alcohol dulled the pain in his arm. The door behind Sid creaked open. He recognized who had come out by the thump of their heavy boots on the wood planks.

"How's the wing?" Mason Klempt said, dropping his bulky frame onto the step next to Sid.

"Had worse."

Mason nodded. He took a rectangular tin from the chest pocket of his sleeveless denim vest. His nicotine stained fingers removed two cigarettes he'd rolled himself. Sid accepted one of the slender sticks.

"Take me through what happened?" Mason said, striking a wooden match to life.

"Am I the first one you're asking?"

"You're the only one conscious."

"Yeah?"

"Docs got your cousins doped up on painkillers. They can barely string a sentence together."

Sid centered the end of his cigarette over the flame. When the tobacco ignited, he inhaled deeply. He closed his eyes then opened them as the nicotine hit his brain.

"Spotted some prick with a dog on the cameras, lurking around at one of the drop sites. Me and the boys went to get him the fuck out of there."

"You talk to him?"

"Yeah."

"What'd he say?"

"Was a hiker, and got turned around. Said he didn't know he was on private property."

"That's all he said?"

Sid shrugged, and inhaled on the cigarette.

"Who threw the first punch?"

Sid shrugged again.

Mason squinted at Sid through the smoke. "You provoked him, didn't ya?"

"He shouldn't have been there."

"For fuck's sake, Sydney. Didn't I tell you to use your head? Don't go looking for trouble. And what do you do?" Mason shook his head in disappointment. "Was he law?"

"Can't say for certain. Had the look to him."

"The fists too, apparently."

Sid scowled. "Fucking dog. If the mutt wasn't there, the asshole wouldn't be breathing right now."

"You better pray to Jesus boy he wasn't the law."

"They would've shown up already if he was." Sid sipped the beer. "Cops can't be on us already. There's no way."

"And what if this guy brings them now?"

"He won't."

"How you know that?"

"He's probably feeling lucky to have left with his life."

"From the looks of it he's not the lucky one."

Sid flicked the smoke onto the step with a sneer. He ground

the butt out with his heel. The drugs were kicking in and he wasn't in the mood for a lecture.

"He doesn't know where we live," Sid said. "Where's he going to bring the cops? An empty field?"

"Uh-huh." Mason spit, and flicked ash from his cigarette. "Take some extra boys with you tonight to play it safe."

"We'll be fine."

"Take them. No discussion on that."

"Sure. Whatever," Sid said, raising the beer.

Mason slapped the bottle out of Sid's hand. "Don't 'Whatever' me, boy." He stood, towering over Sid. "Bring support tonight. Period. Go on and get out of here now before you make me mad."

Sid glared at his uncle, as he rose from his seat. He picked up the beer bottle from the dirt. Using his t-shirt, he cleaned the glass mouth. He finished the dregs as his uncle stomped into the house. An ecstasy of warmth flowed through his veins. *Damn those drugs are good.* He smashed the empty bottle against a rock, picturing the head of the black and tan dog that'd bit him. *Fucking dog.*

Wyler and Blackjack woke in the hotel from a dead sleep at eight at night. Wyler washed his face with cold water, then threw on a fresh shirt. He ordered take-out for dinner. While waiting for the food to arrive, Wyler double-checked the backpack he'd taken into the woods on their maiden voyage. For this trip, he added night vision goggles and binoculars. Once they finished eating, they got in the Bronco, and were on the road by nine.

Wyler drove east, looping his way around through the adjacent state forest. He parked in a secluded section three miles from Mason Klempt's property. Wyler strapped the knife from his backpack to his belt for easy access in case things got hairy again. Since it was a night operation where more things were prone to go wrong, he leashed Blackjack and clipped him to his belt. On his Apple watch, he loaded his map. He affixed the night vision goggles to his head and then threw on the backpack.

"Ready?"

Blackjack barked once. The familiar sensations of excitement, mixed with a respected twinge of fear, reminded Wyler of his days in Afghanistan. Man and dog working in harmony, going into the unknown to root out the world's monsters. Pushing aside his apprehension, Wyler took a deep breath as he and Blackjack seeped into the blackness.

Chapter 10

Their progress through the woods was slow but steady. After the first mile, Wyler and Blackjack grew more confident moving through the terrain. They quickened their pace. When they got to within two hundred yards of the property, they stopped and had a water break. Then they closed to within fifty yards. Wyler crouched behind a fallen tree and surveyed the lay of the land. From where they hid, the barn blocked the view of the other structures on the property. A glow of lights fanned out from around the edges. The lawn lacked trees, so they'd have to approach the barn exposed. However, their position and the minimal light played in their favor. For the next twenty minutes, they didn't move, waiting and watching.

Then they crept to the left, swinging in a wide, slow arch until Wyler had a clear view of the main house. An overhead lamp illuminated a porch spanning the width of the front facade. A man sat on a bench smoking. The windows on the first floor of the two-story house cast shadows of moving figures behind closed curtains. A man strolled out of the front door. He rested a shotgun casually against his shoulder. He spoke to the man on the bench, but Wyler was out of range to hear what they said. After the brief conversation, the man with the shotgun returned to the house. The presence of guns upped the stakes. Crossbows were one thing; guns were another. Five minutes ticked by, but nothing else happened, so he returned to the downed tree behind the barn. Two windows on the right side were his target.

He whispered to Blackjack. "We check it out, then we're gone."

As he was about to break from his cover, Wyler's phone vibrated. A notification. He put his phone low on the ground at the base of the tree to shield the screen light. The notification came from Sid's camera app. Something triggered it. Wyler tapped the notification, launching the app. Two seconds later, the live video feed played.

A truck towing a medium-sized trailer crossed the center of the field where Wyler had beaten three men senseless yesterday. Two more trucks came into view of the cameras moments later. Men stood in the beds of the lone trucks. They turned on spotlights mounted to the roof and angled them toward the opening of the clearing leading to the connecting path. Then they jumped out of the beds and met up with the drivers, forming a loose horizontal line. Wyler counted at least six men. He squinted at one of them in particular. His finger tapped through the cameras, stopping on the one with the closest shot of the figure's face. *Sid.* Another guy held a walkie-talkie to his mouth. *Waiting for something.*

Wyler selected a different camera and spotted a guy leaning against one of the trucks with an assault rifle dangling across his chest. Another stood at the back of the trailer, opening the door. Wyler pulled up another camera displaying the opening to the path. The men shuffled. Suddenly a driverless ATV rocketed into the clearing, skidding to a stop in front of the line of men. Attached to the back of the ATV by short leashes were five greyhounds. Wyler's heart quickened at the sight, knowing he'd hit paydirt. The initial greyhound that had set him on his path clearly was part of something bigger.

The men swarmed the dogs, unhooking them from the leashes and wrangling them by their collars. They corralled the dogs to the back of the trailer and forced them inside. One of the guys waved to the front of the ATV and then spoke into his walkie-talkie. The vehicle then backed up, turned around, and sped away. Wyler looked up from the phone, quickly scanning his surroundings to ensure no one had detected them. Satisfied they were still clear, he returned his focus to the phone. The group hadn't left. Instead, they reformed their line. *Why didn't they leave?* He tapped the map on his watch and calculated how far away he was from the clearing. He and Blackjack could get there in under half an hour if they moved briskly. *But would the gang still be there?* And what would he do when he got there? As confident as he was in Blackjack's and his abilities, a knife and a pair of knuckledusters against assault rifles and handguns didn't give him the greatest of odds. He also didn't know how many other men were inside the trucks.

Wyler held his position. If the group returned to the Klempt property, more of his hunches would be proved right, and he could gather more information. And if they didn't, he could devise a plan of action to hit them at the clearing.

He watched the screen again. Ten minutes passed before the ATV returned with another five greyhounds. Each man carried out their task with the same efficiency level as the first batch. After the dogs were loaded, Sid waved to the ATV again. Wyler guessed a camera had to be mounted to the front of the vehicle. As the ATV maneuvered and then disappeared into the treeline, the rest of the men clambered into their trucks. They were leaving. The whole event took under twenty minutes. On the fourth camera, the trucks headed toward the exit road farthest to the east. When they were out of sight, Wyler closed his phone and pocketed it.

Voices filled the air behind him. People shouting at one another. The glow of lights increased, putting Wyler on high alert. His pulse quickened, as his senses attuned to the shift in the environment. *Something's happening.* A sense of dread filled him then that he had triggered an alarm or a camera he didn't see. His instincts told him to find a better recon post. Wyler crouched and tapped Blackjack as flashlights bobbed around the edges of the barn.

"Come on," he whispered. They moved to the right, staying low, pausing behind a tree every few feet. When the front of the barn was visible, he took cover in some foliage, laying on his stomach with Blackjack doing the same. Three men stood at the door. One of them fiddled with the lock clamped to a massive chain. Once it was free, the other two men slid the doors open, revealing a brightly lit interior. The men didn't show signs of coming into the woods. They focused on their tasks. Wyler's breathing slowed as he reassured himself he and Blackjack were still undiscovered.

Wyler fished out the binoculars from the backpack. The barn's interior didn't match his expectations based on the rural settings. Smooth concrete lined the floor. Rows of bright tube lighting suspended from the ceiling. Three ATVs were parked along the right-hand wall. High-polished stainless steel tables aligned in a row occupied the middle of the barn. Against the left side were two cinder block walls forming a stall of some sort. Drilled in metal loops stuck out at even intervals at knee height. A hose, similar to one at a car wash, snaked over the top of one of the cinder block walls. Another ATV with an open bed trailer hitched to the back was parked near the stall. Wyler panned the binoculars from side to side, unable to spot any other entry or exit points.

The three men who opened the doors walked in and took out supplies from under the tables. They placed scales on the shiny table tops, along with boxes of small plastic bags and latex gloves. When they finished at the tables, one man went to the back of the barn and wheeled a tank, like one used to fill balloons, over to the stall. Then the three of them gathered outside the entrance. Each lit a cigarette, passing around a communal lighter. Five minutes later, the sound of diesel engines rumbled in the distance. Three trucks appeared, and parked along the left face of the barn. The last of which had the trailer with the dogs. The engines died. The trailer opened, and the men filed in, coming out with a dog in each hand. Some of the greyhounds yipped and bucked, trying to free themselves. Blackjack inched forward.

"Easy." Wyler whispered.

Wyler stared through the binoculars again, tracking the first set of dogs. The man led them to the shower stall. Another man clipped a leash on the first dog and strung the tail end through the metal rings. He stepped around the cinder block wall, tightening the slack until the dog was pinned in place. A third man stepped up, turning the knob on the balloon-filling-looking tank. When he picked up the hose, Wyler realized what was happening. His stomach tightened, and his heart raced. He watched helplessly as the man put the end of the hose to the dog's forehead. His hand squeezed, and a loud burst of compressed air rang out as a bolt fired, killing the greyhound instantly.

Chapter 11

The man behind the wall released the tension on the leash, and the dog sank to the ground. A fourth man, wearing a pair of latex gloves, moved into the stall. A butcher's smock covered the man's bare torso. He unsheathed a knife from his hip and crouched in front of the lifeless animal. Wyler battled back a rising wave of nausea as the man sliced open the dog's stomach. The man rooted inside, extracting all manner of gore and tossing it into a large tin bucket. After a few minutes, he held up an object about the size and shape of a roll of quarters. He dropped it into a separate shallow tray that looked like a gold miner's pan. Once he had put three of the rolls into the pan, he handed it off to a fifth man: Sid.

With a grin, Sid disappeared behind the cinder block wall. He reappeared two minutes later, shaking his hands as if he'd washed them. After collecting the rolls, Sid handed the pan back to the man with the knife. Then walked the rolls to the table, where three other guys stood wearing their latex gloves in front of the scales and plastic bags. Sid handed one roll to each of them. They used a knife to make an incision down the center and worked the protective casing off another package. Out of this inner case fell white pills. The men at the stations gathered the drugs and began sorting them into the small plastic bags, occasionally stopping to weigh them on the scales.

Wyler swung back to the stall, where the man with the knife grabbed the dead dog by the collar and tossed its carcass into the trailer attached to the ATV. And with sickening efficiency, the cycle repeated, and the next dog entered the killing stall. Blackjack pawed at Wyler's arm, letting out a low growl. Wyler lowered the binoculars and glanced at his partner.

"I know," Wyler said. Blackjack nudged Wyler with his nose. "I'm sorry, we can't do anything right now. We're outnumbered and outgunned." Another paw landed on Wyler's arm. "I'll figure something out. Don't worry. Stop now."

Wyler didn't watch the rest of the slaughter. Each burst of compressed air took another innocent creature's life like a bullet to his heart. Each burst, the rage inside him grew. Each burst, he committed to making them pay. When the tenth and final sound of death ended, Wyler resumed his surveillance.

The man with the knife threw the last dog carcass into the pile on the trailer. He then had one of the other men spray his hands and knife off with the hose. He dried his hands on the underside of his smock, then moved aside to allow the cleaning of the stall to commence. Sid supervised the packing of the pills at the center tables. Thirty minutes later, the men finished. On the wall at the back of the barn, Sid directed four guys to lift the top off a hay bail concealing a massive safe. He spun the dial and then the lock released. The personalized packets of pills were collected and stored in the dark belly of the safe.

The group cleaned up their stations, putting the barn in order before they trickled outside. Three of them lit cigarettes and hung around while the others headed toward the house. After a few minutes, one of the guys smoking flicked his butt, waved, and got into his truck. The other two meandered away when the truck drove off, disappearing behind the barn.

Wyler considered packing up and leaving when a faint memory came to him. It would require him to get inside the barn, which was risky. He needed leads to uncover the other end of the operation, though, and this was an opportunity. If it was going to happen, he couldn't waste any more time. He quickly unleashed Blackjack, stuffed his gear into his backpack, and slung it on.

"Blackjack, on me."

They rose to a crouch in unison. Wyler checked his direct line of sight one last time. He breathed in deeply and propelled himself forward. He set his pace between a power walk and a sprint. *Move. Don't stop. Stay alert.* His head rotated in continual motion, sweeping in a 180-degree arch for any threats. His ears pricked up like hypersensitive microphones listening for sounds of incoming dangers. Blackjack moved in lockstep with him, an arm's length away. When they reached the inside of the barn, Wyler paused and glanced over his shoulder to confirm no one saw him. Then he crept to the trailer filled with dead greyhounds. The stench of death in its early stages assaulted his nose.

"Watch my six," Wyler whispered to Blackjack.

Wyler grabbed his phone and fired up the camera. He surveyed the dogs and moved to the first one with its head fully exposed. Delicately, as if not to disturb the creatures in their eternal slumber, Wyler lifted the dog's left ear. Using his thumb, he brushed back the hairs and photographed a set of numbers tattooed on the skin. He laid the ear down, then tilted the bloodied face to the side. Wyler lifted the right ear and snapped another picture of the tattoo of a two-digit number followed by a letter. His eyes shot over to Blackjack for an assessment of their situation. The dog stood steady and alert with no signs of agitation. *Keep going.*

To get to the other greyhounds, Wyler had to shift some of them out of the way. As his hands glided under them, their still-warm blood spread between his fingers. He flipped a switch in his mind to go numb to what he was doing, to compartmentalize the horror, the rage, and the sadness as he worked through the corpses. He focused on the task, forcing all other thoughts aside. Two dogs finished. By the fifth, an internal defense mechanism was triggered, making him aware of the time he spent there.

"Anything?" he said.

Blackjack scraped the dirt twice with his front paw to indicate *no*. It was his nonverbal signal for when they were in stealth mode. *Keep going.* Another dog documented, and then another. As he finished taking photos of the eighth dog, Wyler heard a deep growl. He spun to Blackjack, lowering into an attack position. Wyler pocketed his phone without wasting a second and shoved his hands into his back pockets. As his fingers interlocked with his knuckledusters, two men rounded the corner of the barn. One held a red jug of gasoline and the other a shovel. They froze, not expecting to see someone. Wyler didn't hesitate.

"Go," he said to Blackjack.

The dog sprang, attacking the newcomer holding the shovel. Blackjack bit down on the man's arm and rode him to the ground. The man screamed and thrashed, punching at the blur of tan fur. The other man reacted quicker, dropping the jug and reaching for something at the base of his back. Wyler closed the distance in four long strides, getting to the guy as he pulled a gun free of his shirt. A big silver revolver. As the barrel came level, Wyler swung his left fist high and brought it down, connecting at the man's wrist, throwing his aim towards empty space. The gun erupted with a deafening boom.

Not good. The screaming was bad enough, but a .357 going off at close range was sure to bring people to investigate. They needed to move with a purpose. Wyler lashed out with a sharp right-handed jab. The titanium edge of the knuckleduster glanced off the side of the man's cheek, creating a gash in his face. The man stumbled under the impact, raising the revolver as he did, and fired wildly. Wyler dove out of the way of the hail of bullets. The hammer clicked. *Empty.* Wyler leaped up and rushed towards the treeline, yelling to Blackjack.

"Release," he said. "With me."

Blackjack obeyed and raced off after Wyler, catching and surpassing him in seconds. They hit the cover of the woods as a flurry of activity happened behind them. Shouts, lights, and engines fired up as they fled. Someone started shooting next. *Loud even at a distance. A .30/06 maybe.* Wood splintered as bullets lodged into trees. When they covered at least two hundred yards and the lights from the property faded, Wyler took a knee behind a tree. He whistled to Blackjack, signaling him to come back to him. Working quickly, Wyler donned the night vision goggles. When Blackjack returned, Wyler leashed him. And they resumed their escape.

Another hundred yards and the sound of small engines echoed through the woods. *Dirt bikes. At least three of them.* With head-lights, speed, and a better knowledge of the land, the odds of capture were rising against him. The headstart bought him some time, but not the three miles worth he needed to get back to the Bronco. Their pursuers saw the general direction they fled in. *If they were smart, two bikes would go wide, and one would go up the gut. Then the two wide ones would loop back and forth, funneling us into the center.* He could hide and hope they'd give up, but that ran the risk of them bringing more men out to join the search. Plus, the landscape consisted primarily of trees on flat ground, creating a lack of hiding places.

The rattling whine of engines grew louder. At Wyler's current pace, he figured the bikes would catch them in less than five minutes. He stopped and turned, removing the night vision goggles, peering into the night for the flicker of trailing lights. A hundred yards away, he spotted a halo seeping around the trees to his left. Wyler made the decision. He needed to separate the attackers. *Divide and conquer.*

He pulled on the night vision goggles and headed forward but angled his path to the right, planning to draw one of the riders from the group. They covered fifty yards as the engine drew closer. They kept going. Twenty yards deeper into the woods. Sweeping beams of light ricocheted off the surrounding trees. The way the light traveled, two people must have been on the bike—one driving, one manning the light. Wyler released Blackjack from his leash.

"Stay close," Wyler said. "Things are going to happen fast. Attack on my command."

They continued forward another fifty yards when the dirt bike headlight panned across them.

"Here we go," Wyler said. He quickly led Blackjack behind a tree. "Stay."

The light danced madly through the woods, trying to locate Wyler again. He stepped out where they could see him. Someone hooted, and the tiny motor increased its pitch as the driver pegged the throttle. Wyler ran twenty feet before a gunshot thundered out. He slid to a halt, hunching his shoulders and throwing his hands in the air as a show of surrender. The bike whipped past him and made a wide turn, snaking through the trees. Wyler whistled once. When the driver was straight on with Wyler, he gunned the gas, closing to within ten feet. Then the driver jammed on the brakes and jerked the handles, throwing the bike into a skid.

The guy on the back hopped off, holding his high-powered light in Wyler's eyes.

"Woo-eee," the guy said. "What have we got here? A little raccoon scurrying off into the night."

He sauntered toward Wyler with bravado, the glint of a pistol in the guy's other hand. Wyler whistled again, as the guy aimed the gun at his forehead.

"Sammy, if I didn't know better, this boy's whistling Dixie over here."

"Sure sounds like..."

Blackjack dove from the darkness like some sort of demon from hell, cutting off Sammy. Man, bike, and dog crashed to the ground. The guy with the gun spun his head at the commotion.

"The fuck?" he said. With the guy's attention turned to Blackjack, Wyler, in one fluid movement, latched his left palm onto the gun barrel near the front sight and simultaneously drove his right hand into the guy's wrist, tearing the gun clean from him. Wyler took a quick hard step back, creating separation, as he seated the weapon in his hands. Then he pressed the gun out from his chest. Before the stunned guy in front of him could protest, Wyler fired a round through the guy's upper thigh. The guy instinctively clutched the bullet's entry point as he crumpled to the dirt, flinging his light in the process. Screams and growls filled the temporary darkness. Wyler hurried to the light. Once he had it, he focused on the struggle between Blackjack and the dirt bike driver.

"Release," Wyler shouted. Blackjack did as told. "To me."

Once Blackjack was clear of the man, Wyler carefully approached him. The driver clutched his arm while attempting to crawl away, his face frantic yet defiant. Black hateful eyes seethed in the dim light. Wyler walked close enough so he couldn't miss and fired a round into the driver's knee. The man yelled in agony. With the light trained on the writhing men, Wyler holstered the gun in his waistband and removed his knife. He slashed the dirt bike tires and sliced through any visible wires. As Wyler returned the knife to his pack, he donned his night vision goggles again, and then he smashed the headlight against a tree. Without another word, Wyler and Blackjack vanished.

Chapter 12

They continued on an indirect path for at least a mile until Wyler didn't hear any other sounds or indicators they were still being chased. An hour later, Wyler and Blackjack arrived at the Bronco, exhausted and shaky as the adrenaline wore off. Wyler tossed the bag in the back and secured Blackjack in his seat. Wyler drove cautiously and took an out-of-the-way route to avoid possible confrontations if someone was looking for them. How deep the drug operation ran, he didn't know. If local law enforcement were on the payroll, he preferred to avoid them. With the night's events fresh in his mind, he needed to make another call. His GPS led him to a still open convenience store. He paid cash for the new burner smartphone and returned to the driver's seat.

After powering up the burner, he transferred over the photos of the greyhounds from his personal phone. Then he dialed. When the prompts finished, Mack answered on the fourth ring.

"You know I sleep too?" he said.

"You didn't have to answer."

"Didn't expect to hear back from you so soon. Was there a problem with the app?"

"No, that worked perfectly. This is for something else."

"What have you got?"

Wyler tapped on the phone and sent the images to Mack. "You should be getting a set of photos."

"One second." After a pause, Mack said, "What am I looking at?"

"Tattoos inside of a racing greyhound's ears."

"Ok," Mack said. The frenetic clacking of a keyboard in the background.

"Something,my dad told me once," Wyler said. "Breeders would tattoo the ears of track dogs so people couldn't switch them out during a race to prevent cheating or something like that."

"Racing greyhounds in the US get registered with the National Greyhound Association," Mack said, clearly reciting information. "For identification purposes, the dogs get tattoos in both ears early in age. The left ear contains the litter identification number assigned by the Greyhound Association. All greyhounds in the same litter will have this number. The right ear tells the dog's age using a two or three-digit number to make up the month and year. To tell the dogs apart, letters from the alphabet are used."

"And if I remember, databases exist where you can look up the identification numbers and find out information on the dogs," Wyler said.

More sounds of typing. Then Mack said, "Yeah, that seems to be the case. And that's what you want me to do?"

"I need to know where these dogs came from. Who owned them last? I need a name and an address. You can try narrowing the search to Florida. I realize this is a long shot, but if anyone could get that information, it's you."

"It's definitely a long shot, but I'll put it out to some people and see what we turn up," Mack said. "I take it this is another rush job?"

"Yes."

"Ok. I'll get the invoice in and get on it."

"Appreciate it."

"We'll be in touch."

The call ended. Wyler started the Bronco and drove off.

They stumbled into the hotel room a little after midnight. Wyler inspected Blackjack and performed their grooming ritual despite his exhaustion. Blackjack drank some water, then dove onto the bed and was asleep in seconds. Wyler took the gun from his belt and sat at the small table in the room. The gun was a Sig Sauer P320 Compact chambered in 9mm. He removed the steel magazine and popped the remaining rounds onto the table. Twelve remained of the fifteen-round capacity. Striker fire trigger, his preferred style. The gun had a nice size and weight, ideal for concealed carry. Wyler reloaded the magazine and then retrieved a washcloth from the bathroom. Using his knife, he cut the cloth into thin strips. He broke open a hotel pen, and with the ink cartridge and a strip of cloth, he did a cursory cleaning of the barrel. After wiping the gun down, he slid the magazine in and racked the slide, seating a round in the chamber.

Wyler left the gun on the toilet seat while he showered and then placed it on the nightstand before getting into bed. He closed his eyes, but sleep wouldn't come to him. The images of the dead greyhounds kept intruding into his mind. The malnourished bodies. The hole punched into their heads. As he fought away one visual, another would take its place. The memories forced him out of bed, jittery and sweating. He paced the room, trying to control his breathing. The room suddenly felt small to him. Claustrophobic. He needed a distraction.

On his phone, he searched for the nearest casino or poker room. He found one just over the border in Florida, and it was still open for another few hours. Wyler scratched Blackjack's head until his eyes opened.

"I'm going out for a little bit. You rest."

Blackjack sighed and resumed his slumber. Wyler stashed the gun under the mattress and left the room.

The drive to the poker room took Wyler under two hours. He parked away from the dozen cars sprinkled in the large lot. The building rose roughly three stories and lacked any discernible windows. Wyler entered under an overhang leading into an open floor plan. The interior had the faded vibe of a fifty-year-old facility that put little money into upgrades throughout the decades. Light oak flooring cut through lakes of swamp green carpeting. The smell had hints of something chemical to try and mask the years of cigarette smoke that seeped into every porous surface. For Wyler, it was the smell of home. No matter where he went in the world, every casino or gambling parlor exuded, to a certain extent, a similar ambiance. Of the two worlds Wyler drifted between, this was the one he felt the most comfortable in. Gamblers were his people, his kin. The degenerates, the desperate, the hopefuls, and the rare skilled player who ground out some real money were his extended family. Walking in felt like some sort of informal family reunion.

He followed signs until he entered the poker room. A dozen tables filled the vast space. Three tables had games going. Wyler took a corner chair at one with four people playing. He bought into a $2/$5 no-limit game of Texas Hold 'em with five hundred dollars of the money Arlo fronted him for the job. Two of the guys were on the younger side, late twenties, Wyler estimated; another was maybe in his fifties. The fourth guy seated to his right looked upwards of seventy. He wore a scraggly white beard and thin wire glasses that rested on a wide nose. A baseball hat covered a tuft of white hair.

"How you doing?" the guy said.

"Better now," Wyler answered, counting his stacks of chips. "Cards falling good tonight?"

"Eh, maybe for the young bucks," the guy said, nodding at the two twenty-somethings. "For me, about even." The guy faced Wyler. "Name's Duncan."

It wasn't necessary, but Wyler remained in his alternate identity. "Ethan."

"Haven't seen you around here before. Mostly regulars at this time of night."

"I'm in town for a business trip. I couldn't sleep, so I figured I might as well try and win some money while I was up."

"I know how that goes," Duncan said. "What kind of business are you in?"

"I'm a consultant for some private investment firms in the Northeast." He altered his job description to fit the vibe of the table. Anything to make his opponents guess his skill level, he considered a good thing.

"Fancy," Duncan said with a lighthearted grin.

"I don't know that's how I'd describe it."

The hand ended. One of the young guys raked in the chips. The dealer shuffled and dealt Wyler into the game.

"You look military to me," Duncan said.

"Do I?"

"Worked with a lot of them over the years. It's something about the way they carry themselves. Am I wrong? I'm usually not wrong about that sort of thing."

Wyler smiled. "You're not wrong."

"Ha, I knew it. What branch? No, wait, let me guess. Marines?"

"Right, again."

"I told you I was good."

The play stopped on Duncan. One of the young guys said, "Chief, let's go. Bet's to you."

Duncan smiled, peeked at his cards, and tossed them to the dealer. "Fold."

The bet was to Wyler. He called.

"Chief, huh?" Wyler said. "Asks questions and likes reading people, so let me guess...a cop?"

"That's right. Twenty-five years as a State Trooper. Once I retired, I found all my years of training lent themselves to playing poker. I practically live here now."

"There are worse ways to spend retirement."

"That's what I keep trying to tell my wife," Duncan said with a chuckle.

The turn produced nothing worth playing, so Wyler folded. The next three hands, he folded as well but gained insight into their playing styles. The young ones played aggressively, and he got the sense they'd call hands they shouldn't in hopes of bluffing or bullying the more conservative players out of pots. They were Wyler's favorite opponents and the more lucrative ones to play against. The middle-aged guy, whom Duncan referred to as Nate, Wyler pegged as risk averse, would play only strong hands and rarely bluff. And Duncan, Wyler deemed, a solid player but relied too much on talking to try and distract people.

On the fourth hand, Wyler called with pocket tens. A bunch of nothing showed on the flop. He raised to see how his opponents would react, putting his assessments to the test. The young bucks called, and Nate folded.

"I think Mr. Consultant is trying to strong-arm us," Duncan said. "He's either holding some aces, or he's bluffing."

The turn dropped a beautiful ten of clubs onto the felt. Wyler suppressed a smile and checked, baiting his opponents into his trap. The young bucks bet, Duncan called, as did Wyler. A two of diamonds fell on the river. No help to anyone. Wyler had them, so he checked again and got the same results. When the cycle returned to Wyler, he raised. One of the young bucks' eyes narrowed, sensing the trap. Wyler banked on the aggressive style of play, being unable to fold with that much committed to the pot. And he was right. The young bucks called.

"What have you got?" Duncan said, studying Wyler. "Well, it's worth seeing if you're a bullshitter or a shark. I call."

They groaned in unison when Wyler flipped his cards, winning the hand.

"Son of a bitch," Duncan said, shaking his head.

"I got lucky with that ten showing up," Wyler said, scooping in the sizable pot.

"Yeah, yeah."

As the dealer collected the cards, Wyler said, "I noticed a track out there. Are they still running greyhounds?"

"Nah," Duncan said, tilting in his chair. "Florida used to be a hot spot for dog racing. My dad used to take me all the time. In the fifties and sixties, anybody that was anybody would come out to the tracks. But once all these animal activists started screaming about the treatment of the dogs, things weren't the same. They really demonized the industry. Florida held out for a long time, though. It was this last election cycle they passed laws banning it."

"Is that right?" Wyler said.

"Yeah. Put some old-timers out of business. This place had the regular gambling end of things, too, so they came out alright, but the others that only had racing are up shit's creek now. Some people didn't see the writing on the wall."

Stacking his winnings, Wyler said, "What were some of the big tracks?"

"Well, about three I can remember were just tracks. Starlight was one. The Calypso was another, and then there was one near Tampa. I'm blanking on the name, though." Duncan leaned forward as the dealer flicked the cards around the table. "And then there are the breeders. That was big business too. I heard some farms had close to a hundred dogs at a time." He shook his head in disbelief. "Can you imagine that? A hundred dogs, and then you suddenly got no one to sell them to. What do you do with all those dogs?"

Wyler shrugged, thinking to himself, *you don't want to know.*

Wyler played until three forty-five in the morning when the staff started shutting the place down for a four o'clock closing. He cashed out his chips and counted the bills. He had doubled his money. For the time Wyler spent there, he considered it a successful night. He felt good putting his recent tournament loss behind him. The memories slinked back to their dark corners for the time being. Poker had a way of bringing him back into alignment.

Wyler walked out of the building with Duncan.

"You play a solid game there, kid," Duncan said. "I'd say you're welcome back anytime, but my wallet would say otherwise."

"Fair enough," Wyler said with a smile. In the parking lot, they strolled toward the small cluster of vehicles. Duncan pulled a flat circular tin from his shirt pocket. He twisted the top off, pinched a healthy clump of chewing tobacco, and wedged it into the back of his mouth.

"Want some?" he said, offering the tin to Wyler.

"I'm good."

Duncan nodded as he returned the tin to his pocket.

Wyler hesitated for a moment, wanting to ask a few more questions now that they were alone.

"From the sounds of it, you lived here a long time," Wyler said.

"Born and raised, and lived here ever since. Never saw any reason to leave. If it wasn't for the goddamn hurricanes, this place would be paradise on earth."

"I don't know how you live with the humidity. I need the cold every now and again to balance things out."

"Ah, humidity's good for the skin. Helps you live longer."

Wyler laughed. "If you say so."

Duncan spit a brown wad of tobacco juice from his mouth.

"Let me ask you something," Wyler said. "When we talked about the greyhound tracks earlier, were any of the owners... connected?"

Duncan glanced at Wyler with a curious yet suspicious eye.

"Connected?"

"Yeah." Wyler shrugged. "Any rumors of owners working with people who existed in the gray areas of the law."

"Uh huh," Duncan said, spitting again. "What kind of consultant did you say you were again?"

"The kind that protects people's interests by getting them all the information they need."

"And they want to know about racetracks?"

"Listen," Wyler said, lowering his voice to a conspiratorial tone and leaning closer to Duncan. He decided to take a chance with the man and see what he knew. It surprised Wyler how easily and quickly he was able to lie. "The people I work for have their eyes on scooping up any of these failing race tracks for a steal of a price." His read of Duncan guided the story he told, sensing the man enjoying being trusted with secrets. "The only thing is, they don't know all the connections of who really owns the places. And they like to operate above board on everything. If there's one organization they fear, it's the IRS, you know? And they worry if the government checks up on their dealings and sees ties to some questionable folks, then it's not good for their business."

Duncan digested Wyler's tale, working the piece of dip with his tongue, then spit again.

"Well," Duncan said. "It's Florida. Like New York, organized crime is part of the state's DNA. You had characters from Cuba and Columbia, and some of the Mexicans coming over, and of course, the Italians were involved. A ton of drugs came through the state. The Feds cracked down on most of that, though." Duncan raised his hat and scratched his head with his thumb. "Tampa still has a degree of that element operating in the area. A lot of it is different now. Technology changed how they move stuff around and how they function. These guys have to get more creative. As far as the tracks went, though, I didn't deal with them on a day-to-day basis."

"I see."

"There was one thing, though, involving the tracks. The guy who owned the Starlight turned up dead one day."

"When was this?"

"A year or two before I retired. So about three years ago."

"And what happened?"

"They found him one morning sitting in the bleachers. His son found him. A bullet wound out the back of his head. A .38 at his feet."

"Suicide?"

"Yeah," Duncan said, then spit. He took a handkerchief from his back pocket and wiped his mouth.

"You think it was?" Wyler said. "Or was something off to you?"

"The detectives searched that angle. During their digging and information from some of their CIs, the guy had major debts. Apparently, he borrowed a substantial loan from the types of people you're talking about. Whatever he put the money into, it went belly up, and he was on the hook for it. I helped follow up on some of the leads, but ultimately there weren't any credible leads to suggest it wasn't a suicide. No one found a note with the body, so the working theory was he offed himself to get out of what he owed."

"That was noble of him."

"Seemed that way at the time, like he might have tried to spare his family."

"He didn't?"

"I wasn't involved with the case much towards the end, but one of my buddies told me they think the son took over where the old man left off. He thought there might have been some money laundering going on once the son was in charge."

"They didn't pursue it?"

"Well, the state started gaining steam on banning the sport altogether, and finally, they did. So at that point, the gusto to keep probing into it kind of fizzled out."

"Does the son still own the track?"

"I couldn't tell you."

"You wouldn't happen to remember the name of the father and son, would you?" Wyler said.

Duncan stuck his index finger and thumb into his mouth and snatched the tobacco. He looked at it a second before lobbing it away.

"Yeah," Duncan said. "The family name was Judge. The father was Tyler, and the son's name..." He spit one final glob of dark brown liquid. "...was Clayton."

Chapter 13

Enzo Crippa gazed at the ocean from his seat on the outdoor patio of one of the many restaurants he owned. If crime hadn't been so deeply ingrained in his DNA, he would've been a chef. He learned to cook from his grandmother. She taught him the old ways of cooking. Meals that took an entire day to prepare and make. She was tough on Enzo, but she was fair, and the fact she confided her secret recipes to him meant a great deal. But cooking for hours with the demands of a life of crime were constantly at odds with one another. He wished he had a choice in which path he went down, but after he killed a man during a robbery, his path was picked for him. When he ascended to a high-ranking position in the Toro Crime Family, he bought up failing restaurants and turned them around as legitimate businesses. They became his small consolation prize for a life never lived.

An espresso and a freshly baked cheese danish rested on the table in front of him. From his flask, he poured a splash of rum into his black drink. He sipped from the cup, savoring the bold flavors. Movement caught his attention. He turned to the door as two large bodyguards walked onto the patio, their eyes darting around the area for anyone looking to do harm to their boss. After deeming it safe, they stepped aside.

Nico Toro strutted out next. He was taller, with a slight hunch of old age. He walked with a limp he developed after one of the two attempts on his life. A piece of shrapnel from a car bomb severely damaged his left knee. He wore a white linen suit over a blue button-down and no socks beneath a pair of tan boat shoes. The suit was tailored in a slim-fitting style that complemented his thin frame.

Enzo stood as a sign of respect as Nico approached the table. The two men shook hands before settling into the seats.

"Can I get you something?" Enzo asked.

"That espresso looks good."

Enzo whistled, and a young waiter appeared at the door. He took the order from Enzo and then hurried off to fill it.

"So, what brings you by?" Enzo said, forcing a smile. The two men had a long history together, and a sudden appearance generally came with bad news. He replayed the last few weeks. Nothing Enzo did stood out in his mind that would jeopardize putting him in a watery grave. But in his world, it didn't take much to mark someone as a dead man.

"I got a call late last night from Mason Klempt," Nico said.

"Ok."

"Do you know why the boss of the Bama Boys is calling me directly?"

Enzo shifted uncomfortably in his seat. As he sipped his espresso, he glanced at Nico's bodyguards for signs of a weapon being drawn.

"No," Enzo said.

"Apparently, there was an incident last night at Klempt's place."

"This is the first I'm hearing of it. What happened?"

"He said some guy was snooping around in the barn. Said two of his men got shot during a chase."

"Someone tried knocking the place off?"

"They said none of the product or cash they kept there was touched."

Enzo raised an eyebrow. "Really? So what was the guy after?"

"I don't know. They didn't catch him."

The young waiter returned and set the espresso in front of Nico.

"Do you need anything else?" he asked.

The two men shook their heads, and the waiter left.

"Mason went on to tell me three of his men got the shit kicked out of them two days before this at the drop-off spot. According to his men, the guy that beat them up was the same guy at the barn."

"How do they know that?" Enzo said.

"A dog."

"What do you mean a dog?"

"This mystery man had a dog with him both times."

Enzo mulled the information over as he took another sip of his espresso.

"So, who the hell is this guy?" Enzo said. "Doesn't sound like a cop or the Feds to me. Another crew maybe, probing or gathering intel for some kind of move."

"I don't know," Nico said, gently spinning his cup of espresso. "But that's beside the point. Your little operation doesn't sound as foolproof as you sold it to me or Klempt. No one would know what was going on. Layers of insulation. Weren't those your words? To me, it sounds like things are going off the fucking rails. Mason's pissed, and I don't blame him. Five of his men busted up, and he doesn't know why. This operation of yours was supposed to be simple. He wants blood and wants to shut the whole thing down."

"I never knew Mason to be scared."

"Careful, Enzo."

"Come on, Nico, what's this about? I got the timeline moved up substantially. The product came through. We've gotten no indicators from any of our bought-off people in law enforcement that we've been compromised. And yes, this setup still keeps us insulated. We move the drop location, randomize the drop-off days further, and we stay on track making money. That's still the goal, isn't it?"

Nico smiled. "Enzo, you're the best earner I've ever met, and I admire your creative abilities to squeeze people for all they're worth. But sometimes, you've got to cut your losses. This guy, Judge, you gave him a chance, which, if it were me, I would've put a bullet in between his eyes and called it a day after the tracks closed. Now, though, he's becoming a liability. It's time to close it down and him with it as a show of good faith for the troubles Mason's had to deal with. We don't need issues or bad blood with the Bama Boys."

"I get that, but this is an easy fix."

"Unless whoever's nosing around is taken off the map, I think your other ideas will fall on deaf ears."

"This guy can be anywhere. We know nothing about him."

"All the more reason to close things down."

Frustrated, Enzo produced his flask and poured more rum into his espresso. Nico often complained about the difficulties of moving product. So, Enzo took it upon himself and worked out a solution. A solution Nico agreed to. *And now, there's a minor speed bump, which was expected for a new way of doing things, and he wants to 'close it down'. It was stupid, flawed thinking. They were giving away easy money. But Nico and Mason had arrangements, and disagreeing too overtly was a quick way to wind up dead.* Knowing Nico's decision wouldn't change, Enzo attempted to salvage what he could.

"We've got product scheduled to arrive today. Clayton's already been informed of the dropoff. He's the kind of guy, if we cancel, he'll get spooked. And he's a civilian at the end of the day. We don't want him thinking his only option is to talk to the Feds." Enzo shifted in his chair, sitting forward. "Besides, I think it's unwise to bail on our supplier right now. That's an unstable alliance as it is. So we're going to honor the agreement one way or the other."

Enzo paused, thinking. "Another drop is already set for tomorrow with the Bama Boys. Can you at least convince Mason to take one last shipment so we don't have to sit on drugs we can't easily move? Have the drop be at a slightly different location? After that, we shut it down and take Clayton and his half breed cousin off the grid. It's a good way to keep those two from taking off on us. Close this thing out clean."

Nico drank his espresso as if he were downing a shot of whiskey. He took in the view of the ocean and said, "I can see if Mason's open to the idea. And if he isn't…" Nico faced Enzo. "I hope I can trust you to do what's needed."

Enzo returned his stare and nodded. "You know you can."

Nico studied Enzo's face a moment longer, then he smiled. "Good." He rose from the table. As Enzo started to rise, Nico said, "Don't get up. I can see myself out. One of the boys will let you know Mason's decision."

Enzo nodded again. Nico walked past his bodyguards, and then they filed in behind him. When he was alone again, Enzo sighed and poured another shot of rum into his empty cup. With a quick tilt of his head, he drained the warm liquor. As his attention drifted to the vast ocean, his mind ran scenarios of how he was going to kill Clayton Judge.

Clayton woke to the sound of shattering glass. He sprang out of his bed, fully clothed, and grabbed Jed's revolver he had stashed under his pillow. With the gun raised in front of him, Clayton moved into the hallway. Creeping forward, his breath held, he lunged into the kitchen, ready to fire.

"Don't shoot," Jed shouted, raising his hands in defense. He was on all fours, cleaning the shards of a broken coffee mug.

Clayton lowered the gun. "For fuck's sake, Jed."

"Sorry, I didn't mean to wake you," Jed said, resuming his cleaning. "I just wanted a cup of coffee."

"Leave it. We'll get some on the road."

"Where are we going?"

"To get more dogs."

"Where are you getting more dogs from?"

"We're going to see Ray."

"Ah, Clayton, come on. You're going to go see that lunatic? I thought Burt said he fed all his dogs to his alligators."

"Well, Burt's a fucking moron that'll believe anything. I called Ray last night, and he told me he had fifteen we could take. Since it's Wednesday, we can pick up the dogs from Ray, then we can go right to getting them loaded again with product for the next drop tomorrow."

"That's something, I guess. Would put us at forty five total. Halfway there."

"And Ray won't try to extort us like that bastard, Burt. Ray's nuts, but he still lives by some creed of honor amongst thieves."

Jed nodded. He stood and tossed a collection of broken glass into the trash. Clayton could tell he wanted to say something.

"What is it?" Clayton said.

"If we do all this, and the debt gets worked off," Jed said, as he shrugged. "I don't know. Do you think they'll let us stop?"

Clayton looked at his cousin, considering the question. It was one he'd spent sleepless nights thinking about himself. However, he didn't have time to dwell on the future right now. *Put out one fire at a time. Deal with the rest as it comes.*

"The sooner we finish this up, the sooner we can worry about that," Clayton said. "Give me ten minutes. I'll meet you at the truck."

Clayton returned to his room and threw on some fresh clothes. Meeting with Ray made him uneasy, but he didn't have many options. Having forty five dogs, minus the first batch of ten, would buy him at least another week. Clayton debated bringing the gun with him as a safety precaution against Ray's notorious volatile personality. He remembered one story of someone looking at Ray "the wrong way" at a bar, and Ray responded by jamming a dart into the offending guy's eye. Clayton had no desire to be on the receiving end of something like that. So, he took the gun.

Chapter 14

Wyler's burner phone buzzed on the nightstand. The sound woke him, and he rolled onto his side and answered.

"Hello."

"Tell me you weren't sleeping." Mack said on the other end. "I might have to mark this day in my diary."

"I need to stay beautiful somehow," Wyler said, swinging his legs over the side of the bed and sitting up. He glanced at his watch. The time read two in the afternoon. "Do you have something for me?"

"I hope you can appreciate the magic I work for you and with a record-breaking speed, I might add."

"I'd be nothing without you," Wyler said, laying on the sarcasm.

"Anyway, we processed and cleaned up the images and were able to extract the identification numbers. Then we searched the databases where greyhounds are registered and cross-referenced them against the tracks still in operation over the past five years.

We were coming up with nothing, but then we got a match on two of the dogs. After some more digging, we traced them to a breeder in Florida. A man by the name of Burt Hereford."

"I'm hoping you've got an address?"

"Please, don't insult me," Mack said. "I'm texting you the location of his farm now."

"Does he have a file? Any prior arrests or ties to any crime families?"

"His name came up with a few complaints from animal rights activists for abuse, but his arrest record is clean, at least. I'm sending a link to an encrypted site where you can read a summary of all of my findings."

"You're a legend, Mack," Wyler said. "Thanks for the help."

"Any time."

They ended the call. Wyler jotted down the address from Mack, then pulled up the encrypted site on his phone. As he read through the information about Burt Hereford, something about it didn't make Wyler believe this was the man he was after. But there was no denying the dead greyhound he'd seen in the barn last night had been in Burt's possession at some point. Either way, whether he was directly involved or not, he presented a lead worth investigating.

Wyler took a quick cold shower. After getting dressed, he grabbed the Sig, and inched back the slide, confirming a round was in the chamber. He tucked the gun into his waistband at his hip. Wyler collected the rest of his usual supplies, and he and Blackjack headed outside. They drove an hour, crossing into Florida, where Wyler stopped at a rest area. While the Bronco recharged, Wyler bought food, and they ate. When they finished, Blackjack relieved himself in a patch of trees, and they resumed their trek south.

At six-thirty, Wyler turned down a long road at the address Mack had given him. The road eventually widened into a lot in front of a tired house. He positioned the Bronco facing toward the direction they came from on the off-hand chance they needed to make a quick escape. Looking in his mirror, Wyler assessed the landscape. Aside from the house, a large barn lay a few yards off. Rusting engine parts scattered the ground next to old tractors. A maroon Ford F150 and a Ford Escape were parked close to the house's entrance. An uneasy quiet hung in the air. After internalizing his surroundings, Wyler rolled down the windows, then turned off the engine.

"You wait here," Wyler said to Blackjack. "I'll give the signal if I need you."

Blackjack barked once. Wyler got out and walked cautiously to the front door of the house. He knocked loudly, then took a step back and waited. A few minutes passed before the door opened a crack. A black and blue eye peered at Wyler.

"Who are you?"

"Hi, there," Wyler said. "Are you Burt Hereford?"

"Who's asking?"

On the ride down, Wyler concocted another false identity and reason for being there. If the man wanted to see ID, he'd have to bluff his way out of why he didn't have it. "My name's Jack Cannon. I work for Merrick Pharmaceuticals. I'm looking to purchase some of your dogs. I'm told you breed greyhounds, and from asking around, your name came to the top of the list. Can we talk?"

The door edged open a little further, revealing Burt's face. Both eyes were swollen and bruised. His bottom lip had an ugly split down the center.

"Sure, we can talk, but it's going to be a short conversation."

"Why's that?"

"I've got no dogs left to sell. I unloaded my supply the other day."

"You did?" Wyler said. "Damn. I thought I had a winner here. Is there any chance you remember who you sold them to?"

Burt's eyes narrowed despite the swelling. "Who'd you say you work for again?"

"Merrick Pharmaceuticals."

"What's a pharmaceutical company want with greyhounds?"

Wyler flashed a disarming grin. "There's a lot of hoops to jump through for test subjects for our products. Products meant to help save lives, human lives, mind you. So, my boss sends me out to find...alternate means of collecting subjects. Any help would go a long way."

Burt studied him. As the silence grew, Wyler deployed his next tactic.

"I would certainly pay you for your help too."

Burt's eyes widened slightly. *Got him on the hook.*

"Oh, yeah?" Burt said. "How much would that information be worth to you?"

"For a name and an address, how does three hundred sound?"

"Sounds like you're on your own." Burt started to close the door.

"Whoa, ok," Wyler said. "What about five hundred?"

"Make it a thousand," Burt said, keeping his hand on the edge of the door, preparing to close it if he didn't hear what he wanted.

"A thousand?" Wyler exhaled, rubbing the back of his neck as if Burt's ask was over his budget. His performance wouldn't win him an Oscar, but it was convincing enough. "And you have a real address for me? I need to talk to this guy face to face."

"Yeah, I can tell you exactly," Burt said with disdain.

"How many dogs did you sell him?"

"He took thirty."

Wyler hesitated. "A thousand?"

Burt nodded. Wyler turned around and pulled out a wad of cash. He stripped off the bills, pocketed the rest, and then faced Burt. Wyler held the folded cash up.

"Here's a thousand."

Burt opened the door fully and reached a greedy hand toward the cash. Wyler jerked it back.

"First, write down the name and address," Wyler said.

Burt frowned and then disappeared into the house, leaving the door ajar. Two minutes later, he returned with a scrap of paper.

"This is the guy."

Wyler read the name on the paper and his heart quickened. Scrawled out in pencil was the name Clayton Judge.

"Alright, let me get the cash now," Burt said.

Wyler handed him the money. "Thanks for your help."

Burt quickly thumbed through the bills and smiled when he finished counting. "My pleasure," Burt said. "And if you see that bastard, tell him I hope he rots in hell." And then he slammed the door closed.

Back in the Bronco, Wyler said to Blackjack, "You up for another ride? I think we're onto something."

He barked once.

Wyler typed in the new address on the center console, started the engine, and drove off. *It had to be the guy.* Everything Wyler had learned over the past few days pointed to this man, Clayton

Judge, being the first link in the chain of their operation. As he drove, Wyler tried picturing the type of man he would find. Based on Burt's disgruntled closing remark, Wyler wondered if Clayton was the one who gave him the black eyes. Wyler replayed his conversation with Duncan, the ex-cop turned gambler, and what he had said about Clayton's family. If some sort of financial debt was owed to the mob, and Clayton was resorting to trafficking drugs inside of dogs, then Wyler believed he was desperate. And desperation created dangerous people.

Then, an image of one of the dead greyhounds flashed into Wyler's mind. His hands tightened around the steering wheel, disgusted at the type of people who were ok inflicting that type of senseless violence on defenseless dogs. He was getting close. Each step of the way to him was like lighting matches in a dark tunnel leading to a house of cards. And now that he'd found the right path, it was time for him to burn the whole thing down.

As the sun descended, Wyler approached the address Burt gave him. They had traveled a good two hours outside of Tallahassee and entered into a vast sea of trees. Wyler pulled off to the side of the road a mile from his target. He opened his map on his phone, zoomed in tight, and scanned the area for an observation location. The aerial view on his map showed a house, along with a sizable shed, in the center of a few acres of land. A large pond filled a portion of the front yard. Wyler zoomed out on the map, unable to spot another house for a minimum of a twenty-mile radius. After five minutes of scanning, he picked up on subtle dirt roads cutting through the surrounding woodlands. He settled on the one with multiple avenues of escape but still kept the house in sight.

Wyler drove to the entry point of the dirt road. He watched his location on the GPS until he came to a section he felt was a safe distance away, where he wouldn't be easily spotted but close enough that his high-powered monocular could observe the comings and goings. Then he reversed into the thick of the woods, weaving through the trees until they clustered too tightly together for him to go farther.

In the remnants of the fading daylight, Wyler collected dead branches and created a rough support structure surrounding the Bronco. Using his knife, he then hacked away branches with a healthy amount of leaves on them and layered them horizontally across the frame, camouflaging the rust-colored paint of the vehicle and breaking up the profile of its outline. He worked into the night, stopping only when visibility was too low.

When he finished, Wyler and Blackjack ate a few strips of beef jerky. From his storage, Wyler dug out his Bushnell Night Vision Equinox Z2 monocular, a small tripod, and a power pack. Then he flipped open the rear window.

"Alright, in you go," Wyler said, scooping Blackjack up and easing him inside the Bronco. Careful not to disrupt his camouflage structure, Wyler climbed to the vehicle's roof. He laid flat and screwed the monocular onto the tripod. Then he took out his phone and called up the app that streamed the footage from the device. When the feed came through, Wyler plugged his phone into the power pack. After some panning and repositioning, he zeroed the monocular on the house. With a steady hand, he swept the lens across the face of the single-story ranch. No lights were on inside, and he didn't pick up on any signs of movement. He directed his attention to the shed next. No activity. From the looks of it, no one was home. Another twenty minutes passed.

Not wanting to repeat what happened at the Klempt farm, he settled in for a long night of reconnaissance and waited for his target to show.

Chapter 15

Clayton parked in a lot set amongst rows of mud-crusted trucks. Trash can fires dotted the perimeter, creating a trail. The flames cast the swamplands in an eerie night time glow.

"You ready?" Clayton said.

"I'm not fucking getting out of this truck," Jed said. "Are you nuts?"

"What are you talking about?"

"I know all the stories about Ray, the same as you do. I'm not going out there. The guy scares the shit out of me. You think I want to be on the receiving end of that sadistic fuck? No, thank you. When you get the dogs, I'll come help, but until then, you're on your own. I thought this was a bad idea from the get-go."

"You're seriously going to puss out on me?"

"You're damn right I am. I've heard the stories that happen here. Satanic worshiping and voodoo, and who knows what else. Dark shit you don't want to mess with."

"You're unbelievable," Clayton said. "Those stories are all bullshit to scare people."

"Well, mission accomplished. Fuck that bayou mojo shit."

Clayton shook his head and grumbled. He opened the door and said over his shoulder, "I'll be sure to stop and pick up some tampons for you on the way home, you little bitch."

Jed didn't respond as Clayton slammed the door. Twenty yards away, two men the size of oak trees sat on the open bed door of a massive truck with tires as tall as a full-grown man. Music blared from a speaker behind them. As Clayton approached, one of the guys hopped down from his perch. Through the dim light, Clayton could see the guy holding a machete.

"And who the fuck are you?" the machete man shouted over the buzz of the music.

"I'm here to see Ray," Clayton shouted. "He's expecting me. Tell him Clayton Judge is here."

The way the man glared at Clayton reminded him of a starving person deciding which piece of a filet mignon they wanted to cut into first.

"Hold on," the machete man said. Using a small step attached to the truck's underside, he leaned into the truck's cabin, grabbing a cell phone. After a brief conversation, he hung up and waved Clayton through.

"Go on up," he shouted as he returned to his outpost.

Clayton glanced back toward Jed in their truck, and considered bailing. His palms were drenched with sweat—an agitating ringing in his ear. *Or was he imagining that?* He spat on the ground. *What difference did it make? If he couldn't come through for Enzo, he was as good as dead anyway.* He walked to the house, which was constructed from three shipping containers. Two conjoined on the short sides to form the first floor, and the third stacked on top, creating the second floor. An assortment of windows were cut at odd intervals into the siding. Heavy metal music pumped from the house, and a group of people thrashed to the sounds in a small moshpit. Their stage consisted of a plywood porch propped up by cinder blocks.

Clayton slipped past the flying limbs and entered the first floor through the wide front double door. The volume of the music vibrated against the walls and pounded inside Clayton's skull. He didn't know where Ray was, so he picked a random direction and set off. In the first room he came across, he found four guys shooting up what he guessed was heroin. In the next, were people in the midst of a threeway. He stumbled out of the room and navigated into a kitchen. Two guys stood by an open window drinking 40s and smoking weed. Each had beards stretching to their chests, and leather biker vests loosely covered their bare chests.

"Ray around?" Clayton said.

Neither of the men immediately responded. Then the one on the right flicked his cigarette butt into the dirty sink and glanced at his wristwatch.

"The show's about to start. He's probably up on the deck. Come on with me," the bearded guy said. He disappeared out of the kitchen. The other man stared Clayton down as he left the room. They walked down a hallway until they reached a set of stairs bolted into a side wall. On the second floor, couches, chairs, and coffee tables packed the room. People in various stages of a drug high slouched on the furniture. Nauseating scents of weed, spilt beer, and burning rubber wafted through the air. A bar filled the far back wall. To Clayton's right, floor-to-ceiling glass doors were open, leading onto a raised deck. A dozen men stood next to the railing, looking down at something.

In the corner, a man holding a megaphone climbed onto a waist-high platform. The man was average in height with a lean muscular physique. His brown hair was tied in a tight ponytail. He wore only a pair of cargo shorts and nothing else. Every inch of his chest was a canvas of tattoos. His skin resembled a reptile from his lifelong obsession with the sun. He was the man Clayton had come to see.

"That's him there," the bearded man said.

Ray plucked a cigarette from his thin lips before speaking into the megaphone.

"Ok, you fuckers and degenerates, all betting is now closed. It's showtime."

Cheers and hoots roared from the onlookers. Clayton pushed into the crowd for a better view of what was happening. Below the deck, a thick barred fence formed about a thirty by thirty-yard enclosure. Ten yards of dry land stretched out from the shipping container house before submerging into a black sheet of murky water. Tiki torches strapped to the fence lit the area in a hellish haze. The sound of a chain rattling came from under the deck. A goat appeared on the patch of land. The onlookers cheered at the sight.

"The clock starts now," Ray bellowed into the megaphone.

A large digital clock affixed to the back fence flashed to life. The numbers began counting. Someone behind the goat used a long metal pole to prod the animal toward the waterline. The goat bleated in protest. As it got closer, something in the water moved, creating a steady ripple. The men cheered louder. When the goat was five feet from the edge, the man prodding it quickly retreated. The goat stood in place and bleated more. Then the water went still again. The noise of the crowd dulled to a hush in anticipation. Clayton watched dispassionately, having never cared much for animals.

An alligator burst from the water with a terrifying suddenness. Its long prehistoric jaws flung wide, revealing its uneven razor teeth. The jaws slammed closed, missing the goat by inches. The action whipped the onlookers into a frenzy. They screamed and shouted at the alligator. The goat fled, darting back to the fence. The alligator slithered onto the dry land and stopped, assessing where its prey had gone. In a slow, steady progression, the alligator forced the goat into the corner of the fence, clearly trying to lead it back toward the water. With no place left to run, the goat retreated to the edge of the black pool. The alligator closed in. When it was within striking distance, it lunged forward. The goat dodged the attack, moving to its left. It made it all of three steps before another alligator broke from the water, clamping its powerful jaw around the goat's leg. Cheers, mixed with groans, came from the crowd then. The alligator reversed into the water and, with a barrel roll, dragged the goat under.

"That's time," Ray shouted into the megaphone. "Clocking in at six minutes and twenty-nine seconds. The over-under was at five minutes. Winners collect their bets at the bar. Losers, better luck next time."

The onlookers dispersed, and Ray hopped off the platform. Clayton made his way to him through the crowd.

"Ray," Clayton shouted.

Ray turned, peering at Clayton through a fog of cigarette smoke. It took a minute for his eyes to recognize who was talking to him.

"Clayton Judge. As I live and breathe," Ray said, extending his hand for Clayton to shake. As Clayton accepted the greeting, he wondered how many people those hands had killed.

"What did you think of the show?"

"It's something, alright," Clayton said.

Ray grinned with pride. "Damn straight. Come on, let me get you a drink."

"Listen, Ray, if we can, I'd like to get the dogs and be on my way. I'm on a schedule."

The grin on Ray's face flipped to a frown. "You're going to refuse your host a drink?"

"I mean no offense by it. I'm under the gun a bit."

"Under the gun? You mean like this?"

With a blur of speed, Ray produced a snub nose revolver from the small of his back and pressed the barrel under Clayton's chin.

"That's what I call under the gun," Ray said.

Frozen in place, Clayton stared into Ray's wild eyes. He wanted to puke, but showing fear would only make things worse. Clayton swallowed. "Are you done?"

Ray pressed the gun further. *Was this how his father felt before killing himself?* Warm metal wedged into his flesh. The twitch of a finger all that stood between living and dying. As much as Clayton hated his father, he respected him for having the guts to pull the trigger. Clayton knew he could never do it, but if this was the end of the road, he wished Ray would get it over with already.

"Shit, you've got some stones on you, boy," Ray said, smiling, as he pulled the gun back. "If you're all about business, then fine, let's do some business."

When Ray turned, Clayton wiped the sweat from his forehead and followed. He'd just passed one test, and he prayed there weren't more. They picked their way through the house and exited a concealed side door on the first floor. Ray walked with a purpose over the grounds, moving farther into the darkness of the night. As the music faded, it was replaced by sounds of unknowable creatures lurking in the shadows, waiting for the right moment to claim his soul. Every fiber of his being couldn't wait to be gone from the place. Eventually, Ray stopped at another shipping container, partially sunken into the ground. They climbed a short ladder to the top. Ray grabbed hold of a handle and pulled open a metal door.

"Go ahead," Ray said, stepping out of the way. "You first."

Clayton hesitated, then moved to the open space, peering into the container's belly, lit by a single bulb. *Test number two.*

"What's in there?" Clayton said.

"Only one way to find out."

Clayton paused a moment longer, then took a deep breath and lowered himself inside. As he descended another ladder, motion sensor lights flickered on. At the bottom, he turned to see the walls lined with cages—some metal, some glass—filled with animals of every shape and size. Snakes, lizards, birds, fish, and a dozen other creatures Clayton had never seen before, stirred to life at their appearance.

"Jesus," Clayton said. "What is all this?"

"My new business," Ray said. "I knew it was only a matter of time before tracks started closing and the greyhound breeding business was gonna go belly up. So I diversified. Florida's got all sorts of exotic species of animals eccentric rich people want. The harder the critter is to find, and the rarer it is, the more money they'll pay. Fucking rich people, I swear to god."

As they moved farther into the container, the space opened

into a second container completely buried underground.

"Damn, Ray, how many of these containers you got under here?"

"Shit, I got eight of them. I started building all of this way back after 9/11. Took me years to get this the way I wanted it. Got me a full bunker down here too. When the end times come, I'll be ready, brother."

"I think that's an understatement."

They moved past the exotic wildlife in captivity and walked down a set of steps into the second container, where more animals lived.

"You called me just in time," Ray said. "I was about to use them all up for my little gambling show."

He stopped in front of a large caged-in section where the greyhounds were corralled.

"I told you I had fifteen, but when I counted this morning, I only had twelve. I guess I forgot a few went to the gators already."

"How much?"

"Make me an offer."

Clayton rubbed the back of his neck. "I bought some off Burt Hereford for fifty a dog two days ago."

"Burt Hereford sold you dogs for fifty bucks?" Ray laughed. "I don't believe you. He's one of the cheapest, slimiest mother fuckers around. He'd extort his grandmother if he had the chance. Fifty bucks. Get the fuck out of here."

Clayton grinned. "Well, I persuaded him into giving me a good deal."

Ray glanced at Clayton, then grinned. "Son of a bitch. I didn't take you for that kind of a man, Clayton. Boy, what I wouldn't have done to see his face."

"He's a coward at his core."

"True that," Ray said. He stared at the dogs, then said, "How about this, you take ten, leave me two for my gators, and we do a hundred a dog. A grand flat."

When Claytond had gone to see Burt, he expected to pay six grand, close to all of the cash he had available. And now, for forty dogs, he had spent only twenty-five hundred. *Things might be looking up.* He shook Ray's hand on the spot and said, "Deal."

"So, what do you need them for?"

Clayton shrugged as he counted out the payment. "I've got my reasons."

Ray grinned again. "Those reasons got something to do with the Bama Boys?"

"Where'd you hear that?" Clayton said, slightly surprised.

"I'm a people person, Clayton. People talk to me. They tell me all sorts of things."

Clayton swallowed hard, nervous Ray would try shaking him down like Burt. Only this time, he didn't stand a chance of beating a better deal into Ray. Sensing Clayton's hesitance, Ray said, "Listen, I don't care what you do with them or what you got going on with those boys. I like taking drugs, not selling them. As you can see, I've got my specialty going on here."

"Yeah."

"Sounds like they got their hooks in you. How'd they get you?"

"My old man."

"Last I heard, he'd blown a hole through his face," Ray said, then added. "No disrespect."

"None taken. He was a rotten son of a bitch who took the coward's way out," Clayton said. "But the Bama Boys aren't the problem. It's the Toro family's thumb I'm under."

"Ah."

"The old man took a loan from them he couldn't repay. So, when he died, they put it on me. We were laundering through the track, but now that's gone, and I don't have a pot to piss in and can't pay, I've got to work it off."

"So you're moving product through the dogs?"

Clayton nodded.

"That's clever."

"My old man loved these fucking dogs more than me, so I see it as a final fuck you to him."

Ray laughed and slapped a hand on Clayton's shoulder. "You got that cold blood running through your veins, Clayton. It's a sentiment I can appreciate. How's that saying go? You can't pick your family or some shit."

"Sounds about right."

"Well, let's get you on your way then." Ray opened the gate with the dogs and got leashes on them. They took five dogs apiece. "Come on this way."

Clayton followed Ray down a corridor until they came to a dead end.

"Hold tight," Ray said. He kicked a lever, and the ground beneath them rose. The ceiling folded open, and the mechanical lift ascended, stopping once they were above ground again.

"Pretty cool, huh?" Ray said, stepping off the platform.

"Bet that wasn't cheap."

"Shit, money won't mean a thing when the end times come, brother. It was worth every goddamn penny."

They continued in silence, wrangling the dogs through the darkness. A few minutes later, the truck came into view. Jed jumped out to help load the cargo into the trailer. He avoided eye contact with Ray and hurried to get the dogs secured. When they finished, Jed got back in the truck without a word uttered.

"Kid seems kind of squirrely," Ray said.

"He was born that way, unfortunately," Clayton replied.

The two men grinned and shook hands.

"Well, good luck to you," Ray said. "Don't let your guard down around those pricks."

"I'll try not to."

Clayton climbed into the truck and reversed down the driveway. His muscles relaxed as Ray's hellscape of a compound shrank in the distance of his rearview mirror.

Chapter 16

As the night wore on, Wyler drifted in and out of sleep on top of the Bronco, waiting for Clayton's return. Around one on Thursday morning, Blackjack made a noise, alerting Wyler. He tapped on his phone and fired up the monocular. Swinging it through the trees, Wyler spotted movement. A Chevy came to a stop in front of the house. The driver—a man, on the shorter side, with a weightlifter's build—got out and crossed the lawn towards the shed. Wyler panned the lens. Another smaller and skinnier man opened a trailer attached to the back of the truck. The smaller man disappeared inside the trailer, and a few minutes later, he emerged holding two greyhounds. He dragged the dogs using ropes around their necks. The man forced the dogs to the shed, where he handed them off to the bigger guy.

Wyler pictured Burt's beaten face. If one of these guys did that to him, he bet on the bigger one being responsible. Wyler put his money on him being Clayton Judge. They continued to unload the trailer. When they finished, Wyler had counted ten dogs. If Burt sold Clayton thirty, but ten were killed, and now another batch of ten arrived, Wyler assumed there were at least thirty dogs in the shed. Satisfied he had his man and the other end of the operation, Wyler left the monocular running and climbed into the back of the SUV with Blackjack.

"I think we've got our guy," Wyler said.

From the cabin, he grabbed the burner phone and punched in a number. After the other line rang a few times, a woman's voice answered.

"Hello," she said. "How may I direct your call?"

"I need to speak with my advisor about the ETF DEC," Wyler said, reciting the code Arlo had given him as a way to get in touch through a secure connection.

"One moment, please."

The line went silent, then ten seconds later, Arlo answered.

"Declan. I was expecting to hear from you sooner."

"I wanted to have everything lined up before I reached out."

"I take it you've found something then?"

"I think so."

"What have you got?"

Wyler took Arlo through the past three days; making contact with Hudson, finding the clearings, and the run in with Sid and his crew.

"I see," Arlo said. "And are they still in the land of the living?"

"They are, but they won't forget us anytime soon."

"Go on."

Then Wyler told him about the security cameras, and how he followed a lead to the Klempt property. Wyler paused, remembering the night and what he had witnessed. He thought of how to frame it for Arlo. Sensing his hesitation, Arlo said, "Give it to me straight. I need to know."

"Whoever is involved, I can confirm they're using greyhounds to traffic drugs. Fentanyl, to be precise."

"And what happens to the dogs after they've played their part?"

Wyler sighed and then lowered his voice. "They get terminated."

Arlo didn't respond immediately. Then he said, "Understood."

"There's more."

"Let's hear it."

"I lifted tattoo photos from the greyhounds' ears and sent those to Mack. He got a hit on them leading me to a breeder who recently sold thirty dogs to a man named Clayton Judge. From what I've pieced together, this guy is doing this to work off a mob debt. I'm staking out his property right now, and he just brought in another ten dogs. I'm pretty sure this is the man on the Florida end of this operation."

"How many dogs total does he have?"

"I'm not concrete on a number yet, but at least thirty."

"Any idea of why they're running it where they are?"

"Nothing I can prove. Based on the map ariels and the fact they used a driverless ATV to run the dogs across, my hunch is they're doing it in part to try and skirt a federal prosecution in case they get caught."

"How so?"

"That's a lot of land law enforcement would have to cover to catch both sides in the act. If they catch one side in Florida, but not the Alabama side or vice versa, then they've got work to do to prove the drugs crossed state lines," Wyler said. "And technically, no human is crossing the border, so if they've got good enough lawyers, they maybe could argue for a state prosecution instead of federal. I'm no lawyer, so who knows if that would actually work, but that's my theory anyway."

"I wouldn't be surprised. People have tried dumber things before."

"The dogs are a solid cover. This guy, Clayton, was involved with a racing track in Florida, so if he got stopped, unless someone ratted him out, what cop would think the dogs were packed with drugs."

"What will these people think of next?" Arlo said, his voice a mix of anger and disappointment.

"I don't know, Arlo," Wyler said. "But it needs to stop."

"What can I do?"

"I'd keep someone on standby for transport. I've got a plan to get the dogs out of here, but I'd need to transfer them at some point. They'll need medical help on the way too."

"I'll work on putting together a small team and get them down there as soon as possible."

"I'm going to send you coordinates of where I am and the locations of all the other people involved. If something happens, you can pick up where I left off."

"Do you want me to call in someone else for support?"

Wyler looked at Blackjack. "It's two guys we've got to deal with. We should be able to handle it. I don't want you to involve anyone we don't need to."

"Ok. I trust your judgment. I'll be on the lookout for the coordinates in the meantime. Keep in touch for where and when you need the transport."

"I will," Wyler said. "And Arlo..."

"Yeah?"

"If push comes to shove with these people, how far are you

comfortable with me taking it?"

Arlo went quiet for a moment. Then he said, "I've got your back no matter what. Shove as hard as you see fit."

"Even if it shoves them underground?"

Arlo went quiet again. Then he said, "Even if it shoves them into the deepest darkest hole."

Chapter 17

Nine hours later, Enzo's driver parked the black Cadillac SUV on the street a few doors down from his restaurant. As a force of habit from being in the crime business for so long, he surveyed the surrounding streets for signs of lurking hitmen before getting out of the vehicle. His driver, who doubled as a bodyguard, met him on the sidewalk, and they headed to the back entrance of the building.

As they approached the door, a man stepped out from the alcove. Enzo recognized him as one of Nico's top lieutenants, Jimmy Ricci. Jimmy tucked a vape pen into his pocket as Enzo approached.

"Jimmy," Enzo said.

"How you doing, Enzo?" Jimmy said.

"I woke up to see another day, so I can't complain."

Jimmy laughed. "I know what you mean."

"What can I do for you?"

"The boss wanted me to tell you the thing with the Bama Boys is a go for the shipment tonight. And then..." Jimmy leaned in close and lowered his voice as if someone were listening in, which Enzo knew they weren't since he had the place swept for bugs twice a day, but he played along. "After it's done, the two cousins...well, that's it for them. Their services are no longer needed. You know what I mean?"

Enzo nodded.

"And the boss told me they want proof it's been taken care of too."

"Proof?"

"That's what he said."

It seemed excessive to Enzo. The added step said to him Nico didn't trust him, but he didn't argue the point. "Ok."

"And that's it," Jimmy said, slapping Enzo on the arm and flashing a smile.

"Thanks for the message," Enzo said, brushing his arm of any residue Jimmy left behind. *The kid has balls.*

"I'll see you around."

Jimmy nodded at Enzo and his bodyguard, then walked away. Enzo sighed as he took out his keys. He still felt the decision was short-sighted and a missed opportunity to move product. And Clayton was the type of person Enzo could extort to do his bidding for years. *What a waste.* He needed to stop dwelling on it, Enzo told himself. Decisions were made and they were final. If he wanted to keep breathing, then he needed to accept those decisions and move on. Enzo inserted the key into the lock and opened the door.

Inside, he switched on the lights and headed to the kitchen. He arranged the items needed for making espresso while considering who he'd send to dispose of Clayton and his bumpkin cousin. Enzo wasn't opposed to violence but preferred to use it as a selective tool when a specific message was needed. Whereas his counterparts—from the old-school generation—used murder a little too liberally. If killing was required, Enzo liked to use the best. Some people he knew wanted to spend as little money as possible on a job or give it to a newcomer, but Enzo had seen that go wrong too many times. For him, paying more for a flawless execution was worth the added expense. He would give Lucian a call. As a former officer of the Italian Gruppo di Intervento Speciale or GIS, Lucian had come under investigation in Italy for unsanctioned executions and several corruption charges, which forced him to flee to the United States. His resume spread through the underworld, making him a highly sought-after freelancer known for his thorough work. Enzo had employed his services twice before with satisfactory results. The only problem Enzo could foresee was the short notice. He'd offer up extra cash to entice him.

After Enzo finished making his espresso, he sat at the empty bar and called Clayton first. On the sixth ring, Clayton answered.

"Hello?"

"It's me," Enzo said. "Is everything set for tonight?"

A few grunts came through the line. Enzo assumed he had woken Clayton.

"Yeah, we're ready."

"Any issue with the product last night?"

"No. We're all good. Another ten dogs are packed as instructed."

"Good. What time are you leaving?"

A pause on the line. Then Clayton said, "We usually leave around ten."

"Alright. Remember, no fuckups. I'll check in tomorrow," Enzo said, knowing there would be no tomorrow for Clayton.

"Alright," Clayton said with a touch of annoyance.

Enzo ended the call. He made a mental note to send one of his boys to watch Clayton today to make sure he followed through. Enzo preferred peace over war and didn't want to risk bad blood with the Bama Boys over someone as insignificant as Clayton Judge. He needed to close the account cleanly. No more mistakes, especially not in the final hours.

Enzo stood and moved behind the bar. He opened one of the small freezers and emptied it of its drinks, placing them on the floor in a neat row. Then he removed the shelves and popped open the back wall. From a hidden compartment, he drew a notebook and a phone. He leafed through the book until he found Lucian's number. He punched it into the keypad and waited. A gravelly voice answered and spoke with a thick Italian accent.

"Speak," Lucian said.

"This is Enzo Crippa with the Toro crew. I've got a job for you. Should be a simple one, but it's on a tight timeline. Can you fit me into your schedule?"

"How tight?"

"Tonight. The target leaves his house around ten and will be back an hour or so after that."

"How many people?"

"Two. They live in a secluded location. No one around for miles."

"Men only, yes?"

"Yes."

"Do they need to disappear? Or is this sending a message?"

"No one will miss them. Might as well make them disappear."

Silence hung on the line. Then Lucian said, "I can do this, but it will cost extra for the rush. Ten thousand on top of the usual fee. Five per head. You agree to this?"

Enzo calculated in his head where he stood on the operation. Overall, he'd be losing out on the unpaid portion of the original debt Clayton's father owed. However, the money he made from the product that did go to the Bama Boys at least covered the price of the hit. Enzo could've extorted work out of Clayton far past what he owed. It was a shame to lose someone with the hook in so deep. *Let it go. Drop it.*

"That's fine. I'll have the advance cash and the details in the usual place by this afternoon."

"Understood. Ciao."

The line went dead. Enzo put the phone and the notebook back into their hiding place and restocked the fridge. He returned to his espresso, pleased with himself for a productive morning.

Wyler came out of a short sleep around eleven. He quickly surveyed his surroundings, ensuring nothing was out of the ordinary. He exited through the back window and then helped Blackjack out so he could relieve himself. While Wyler waited for him to return, he queued up the recorded footage on his phone from the monocular during the early morning hours while he slept. He advanced the footage until it caught up to the present. No signs of activity were captured. He assumed the two people he saw last night were the only ones living in the house. He liked those odds. It made getting the dogs out of there that much easier.

After watching the footage, he inventoried his supplies. If they really stretched it, they had enough water and snacks to get them through about two days. He didn't want to risk leaving and returning to find Clayton and the dogs gone. With that in mind, he figured his best chance was to hit them when night fell. If they left at any point, he could move in earlier, load the dogs, and get out of there. And if they didn't go or they loaded the dogs, then he'd take the riskier route of subduing Clayton and the other guy with him first and then flee with the dogs. He preferred the first option, but his gut told him it would be the second. He prepared himself for either outcome.

When Blackjack returned to the Bronco, they ate outside, then piled back into the bed. Since they had time to kill, Wyler pulled out a book on sign language. Enola had given him the book during the year and a half they had spent together. Whenever he would read through it, he couldn't help but think of her. In the grand scheme of things, they hadn't been together long, but she was one of the few people he had ever truly loved. He pushed aside the nostalgia and opened the book. Enola had introduced the idea to Wyler that dogs could understand and even respond to sign language. Together they worked on it with Blackjack during the tail end of their relationship. When they parted ways, Wyler continued the practice.

He got Blackjack's attention with some treats, and they went through their commands. Wyler progressed with American Sign Language and had slowly developed signals specific to him and Blackjack. They were up to about ten signals Blackjack could respond to in some manner, whether it was how he moved his nose or used his paws. After an hour of practice, Blackjack's attention waned. Wyler put the book away and tried to think of something else.

He turned his attention to how he would subdue Clayton and his partner. Surprise played in Wyler's favor the most. And having the gun helped. Law abiding people did what they were told at the sight of a firearm. However, people on the wrong side of the law were more of an unknown quantity in how they would react. *Would they be armed? How competent were they at close-quarter hand-to-hand combat?* From what Wyler could discern from the monocular, he had both his opponents beat in size. The one he guessed was Clayton looked capable. If Wyler managed to get the drop on them, he would need something to tie them up. He opened his storage compartment beneath the floor and scanned the objects inside. He had paracord, a viable option, but it had drawbacks. After moving a few things aside, he spotted a roll of Gorilla tape.

"Bingo," he said.

While he was in there, he also grabbed a folded ski mask. Sid and his crew had already seen his face, but Clayton hadn't, and he was stealing something directly from him. Wyler figured it wouldn't hurt to wear it as a layer of protection should Clayton get the notion of retribution. With the tape and mask secured, he checked the charge on his night vision goggles and then unloaded and reloaded the magazine of the Sig. He rechecked the footage. No signs of movement.

"Well, boy," Wyler said to Blackjack. "Should get some more sleep while we can. It's going to be a long night."

Wyler laid on his back with the phone resting on his chest should the monocular send him a notification. Blackjack nestled into a ball near Wyler's feet. They were asleep within minutes.

When they woke, it was dark outside. Wyler checked his watch to see it was nine o'clock. He boiled some water with his camping stove and stirred in a packet of instant coffee. As the drink cooled, he checked the footage one last time. No one had come or gone, which meant they were still inside. *Option two, it is.* Ten minutes later, he drank his coffee. Then they climbed out. Wyler holstered the gun on his hip and crammed the roll of tape into his back pocket. He removed the branches from the vehicle since stealth didn't matter anymore. If the operation went south, and they needed to high tail it out of there, he didn't want to have to deal with clearing it in a hurry. When he finished, he donned the ski mask and put the night vision goggles on top.

"On me," Wyler said to Blackjack.

With his partner safely at his side, Wyler pulled out the Sig and flipped on the night vision goggles. And they moved toward their target. After a five-hundred-yard walk, they came to where the main paved road cut a gash through the woods. Wyler stopped and crouched beside a tree. Now closer to the house, he scanned slowly from right to left. The glow of light illuminated a side window. It faded and reappeared as if someone had walked in front of the source. Wyler recalled from the aerial view a grouping of trees to the right provided good coverage to the side of the house where the light came from. He would move in from there and assess how he'd enter the house once he was closer.

As he was about to get up, something snagged in his field of vision to the left. He shifted his body to get a better view. An object that wasn't natural to the horizon line bothered him. With a gentle tap of Blackjack's side, he got up and crept toward the shape. When he got to within twenty yards, the shape's silhouette became defined. A vehicle. He advanced closer. Someone sat in the driver's seat. A tiny bright orb of a cigarette glowed in the night vision goggles. *Who was this? Were they involved with Clayton's scheme? If they were, what were they doing out here? Dark interior, smoking...waiting. Waiting for what? Or were they watching Clayton? The car looked reasonably new, and the driver was too relaxed to be having car problems. Another house wasn't around for miles.*

Wyler hadn't anticipated this new development. *Option one: withdraw, regroup, and return later. But that left the chance for more dogs to be murdered. Option two: proceed as planned and adapt to whatever the person in the car does. Or option three: remove the new development from the equation.*

He chose option three.

Wyler pushed to the left until he was fifteen yards behind the car. The windows were down. He signed a message to Blackjack outlining a plan of attack. Blackjack retreated into the woods, aligning himself with the car's passenger door. With his partner in position, Wyler snuck out from the cover of the trees and dashed on an angle to the trunk. Resting against the bumper, he waited to see if the driver had noticed him. The faint sounds of a sports broadcast came from the window. No exhaust came from the pipe. The car wasn't running. Wyler gripped the gun. *Go.*

Wyler whistled a short and loud signal for Blackjack to move in. As soon as he made the sound, Wyler sprang to his feet and rushed to the driver's side door. He leveled the gun at the driver's stunned face and said calmly but with authority, "Don't move."

The driver stared blankly at the tip of the gun. He regained his composure after the initial shock. The man's hand crept toward his waist. Going for a gun, Wyler guessed. The driver's hand stopped instantly when Blackjack leaped into the passenger seat through the open window. He growled and bared his teeth. The driver pressed his back into the door with enough force Wyler thought he would come spilling out.

"What the fuck?" the driver said, the fear evident in his voice.

"I wouldn't make any sudden movements if I were you," Wyler said. "You don't want to see what my friend here can do to flesh and bones. Do you understand?"

Without taking his eyes off Blackjack, the driver tilted his head toward Wyler. "What the fuck is this?"

"That's what I'm hoping to find out. Now, I want you to slowly lean to the window with both hands on the back of your head. If you try anything, my friend here will sense it and attack. He won't wait for a command if he feels I'm being threatened."

"Yeah, ok, I get it."

"Good. Hands."

The driver raised his hands, his eyes locked on Blackjack. When they made their way to the back of his head, Wyler said, "Interlock your fingers."

The driver complied. Wyler holstered the gun and brought out the tape. He bound the man's wrists together. With his hands bound horizontally, Wyler looped a long strip of tape between the driver's hands, going vertically. Then he threaded the tail end through the back window and brought it through the front window, physically securing him to the vehicle. Wyler tested the strength of the hold. Satisfied, he walked to the rear passenger door, removed his night vision goggles, and got in the backseat. He bent forward and patted the driver down, stopping when he hit something solid. Wyler pulled a pistol from beneath the driver's shirt. *A Glock 19.* He popped the magazine. It was packed to the fifteen-round mark. Easing back on the slide, Wyler revealed the glint of a round in the chamber. He slapped the magazine home and held the gun level on the driver's chest as he relaxed into the seat. When the car's overhead light faded away, Wyler said, "Who are you?"

"Fuck your mother."

"What are you doing here?"

"Suck my dick."

Wyler sighed. "I'm not going to do that, but my friend here hasn't had a good meal in a while." Wyler leaned forward, unbuckled the driver's pants, and unzipped his fly.

"What the fuck are you doing? You fucking little queer. I'll fucking kill you," the driver said as he bucked in his seat, trying to pry his hands free.

Wyler whistled to Blackjack, pointed at the man's crotch, and said, "Bite."

Blackjack lunged forward with a vicious snarl. The driver screamed as Blackjack's nose hit his boxers. "Ok, ok, ok! Fuck! Stop! Stop him!"

Wyler whistled again, and Blackjack stopped.

"Jesus Christ, you're fucking crazy," the driver said. The bravado vanished from his tone.

"Should we try again?"

"Yes, fine. Shit. Just keep that beast away from me."

"Who are you?"

"Gino."

"And what are you doing here, Gino?"

"I was told to watch the place."

"Who were you told to watch?"

"Judge. Clayton Judge. And the little fuck, his cousin, Jed."

"Why are you supposed to watch him?"

"There's a drop tonight, and my orders were to keep an eye on them and make sure they followed through."

"Why wouldn't they follow through?"

"I don't know. I don't ask questions like that. They tell me to do something, and I do it."

"What time is the drop?"

"Boss said he should be leaving sometime around ten."

"And who told you to come watch him?"

Gino moaned. "Come on, man."

"Who?"

"Enzo," Gino said with an air of disgust.

"This Enzo got a last name?"

"Crippa. Enzo Crippa."

"Mafia?"

"What do you think?"

"What family are you with?"

Gino moaned again. "Fuck. Are you a cop? What is this?"

"Your prick is on the line here. You want to keep stalling?"

Gino glanced at Blackjack again, then said, "We're part of the Toro family."

"And who is this drop going to?"

"I think the Bama Boys. A crew in Alabama. But I'm not fully involved with whatever this is. I'm just a footsoldier."

"Do you have to check in with someone at a certain time?"

"No. I was told to call only if there was a problem."

"And what if Judge didn't do what he was supposed to? What were your orders then?"

Gino shrugged. "I was told to follow them wherever they went."

"Is there anyone else out here with you?"

"No."

"Come on, don't lie to me."

"I'm not. I swear."

Wyler contemplated Gino's response. The right pitch of fear and truth was present enough for Wyler to believe him.

"Alright, Gino, luckily for you, you're not my concern. I'll even leave you tied up so you can tell your boss I got the better of you."

Gino shook his head. Wyler sensed the man's sneer through the dark. "They'll come for you. They'll find you, and they'll kill your whole fucking family. And I'll be there to fucking watch."

Wyler extended the Glock forward until the barrel tip pressed into Gino's forehead.

"So, are you saying I should kill you now?" Wyler said.

Gino turned his face to the side and squirmed in the seat. "Fuck...you..." he managed to get out. Wyler bent his arm, then brought the butt of the gun down hard between Gino's eyes. He grunted under the impact, his head lolling in a daze. Wyler put the gun on the seat next to him and then tore off another strip of tape, which he placed over Gino's mouth.

"Stay out of trouble while I'm gone," Wyler said as a farewell to Gino. From the ignition, Wyler plucked the keys and Gino's phone out of the center console. Then he grabbed the Glock and got out of the car. First, he chucked the keys as far as possible into the woods, and the phone followed. Moving to the passenger door, he opened it, and Blackjack hopped out. Without making a sound, man and dog drifted into the woods. With one threat neutralized, they continued to their primary objective.

Chapter 18

Wyler and Blackjack backtracked to their initial entry point to Clayton's property. They darted across the road, entering enemy territory. Wyler checked the time. Five past ten. Their window of opportunity to leverage the element of surprise to its fullest was dwindling. They hustled through the coverage, stopping on the opposite side of the shed. After a brief pause to listen, they advanced. Hugging the wall, they made their way to the back of the shed, where they had a clear view of the house. More lights were on, so Wyler flipped up the night vision goggles.

If the dogs were in the shed and Clayton and his cousin Jed had a schedule to keep, they had to come out soon. He preferred to avoid going into the house as it presented more risk with a floorplan he didn't know. The thought of Gino, though, made Wyler uneasy. The tape secured him, but how long would it hold? If Gino got loose, it presented another unknown quantity to the task at hand. *Going to have to breach it.* His pulse quickened as his senses heightened. For an instant, he was back in Afghanistan about to raid the hut of a suspected Al Qaeda terrorist. Only this time there was no air support. No cavalry to call in. All he had to rely on was his training and the dog next to him, both of which had kept him alive so far.

Side by side, Wyler and Blackjack dashed to the edge of the ranch. Sticking with the Glock, Wyler extended his arms, centering the gun in front of him as he approached the door. He leaned against the house on the side with the door handle, his mind sharp as he lowered one hand toward the knob.

The door kicked open then, and Jed strolled out. The two men, both taken aback at the sudden appearance of one another, didn't immediately move. A split second later, Jed tried to run, but Wyler's reflexes cut him off. Using his left arm, Wyler got Jed in a chokehold and quickly placed the gun against Jed's temple.

"Not a fucking word," Wyler whispered into Jed's ear. Jed groaned under the pressure to his throat, but didn't shout. Wyler felt the man's muscles tensing beneath his grip. They turned in unison to face the door. "Open it." Jed reached out and fumbled to find the handle. When he did, he pushed the door back until Wyler shouldered his way inside. A voice came from down the hallway.

"What the hell was that noise?"

"Search," Wyler said to Blackjack.

Blackjack hurried down the hallway. Wyler propelled Jed after him. A shout came from the room on the left, where Blackjack disappeared. As Wyler got to the room, he spotted Clayton backed against a wall. His hand went for something behind his back.

"Go," Wyler shouted to Blackjack as Clayton brought out the small revolver. Blackjack clenched on the arm and jerked. The revolver roared twice, filling the room with a deafening boom. Clayton abandoned the gun and tried to beat the dog off that was tearing into his flesh.

"Release," Wyler shouted. His ears rang from the gunfire. Smoke and the smell of cordite hung in the cramped space. He kept the gun aimed at Clayton's chest and secured his choke hold around Jed's throat. When Blackjack was at a safe distance, and Wyler controlled the room, he released Jed and shoved him toward Clayton. Without taking his eyes off the two men, Wyler said to Blackjack, "Search." Blackjack turned and left the room to see if anyone else was there.

"Who the fuck are you?" Clayton said between breaths as he clutched his forearm, attempting to stop the bleeding.

"That's not important," Wyler said. He took out the duct tape and lobbed it at Jed. "Use the tape and wrap up your friend's wrists. Wrap some around his forearm too. It'll help with the bleeding."

"I'm not doing that," Jed said, puffing his chest in defiance.

Wyler fired a shot between the two men. They recoiled from the proximity of the bullet zipping past as the wall paneling splintered behind them.

"That wasn't a question," Wyler said.

Jed stared at Wyler, then looked to Clayton for a sign of what to do. Clayton nodded. "Go ahead. Do what he says."

Reluctantly, Jed tore a long strip of tape from the roll and looped it around Clayton's wrist.

"Nice and tight, now," Wyler said.

"We don't have any money here," Clayton said. "You picked the wrong house to rob."

"I'm not looking for money."

"Well, what do you want then? Take a look around. We don't

have shit."

"What about those dogs you got in that shed?"

Clayton's eyes narrowed. "Who are you with?"

"No one you'd know."

"Yeah, right," Clayton said. He winced in pain as Jed wrapped a layer of tape over his wounded forearm. "You've come for the drugs, haven't you?"

Wyler said nothing. A few seconds later, Blackjack returned and sat at Wyler's side.

"We clear?" Wyler asked him. Blackjack barked once.

"I don't know who you're working for," Clayton said. "But if you take those dogs, you might as well kill us now because we're as good as dead."

"That's not my problem," Wyler said.

"I don't think the people you're stealing from will feel the same way."

"I'll take my chances."

Clayton shook his head. A smile spread on his face that turned into laughter. It was a laugh of desperation, hopelessness, and the absurdity of it all.

Wyler ignored him and pointed the gun at Jed. "Get down on the floor. Face first. Interlock your fingers behind your head. Either of you tries anything, and you'll catch a bullet or have your throat ripped open by my friend."

Jed hesitated, scanning the room for any chance at escape. The dog locked on him as if reading his mind. Resigned to his lack of options, Jed went to his knees. As he was about to lie down, Blackjack perked up. A noise caught his attention, and he crept out of the room. Wyler backpedaled until he was in the hallway, where he could see both the men and the dog. Blackjack raised his front paws to a window sill and peered out. After a few seconds, he hopped down and turned to Wyler.

"What have we got?" Wyler asked him. "Visitors?"

Blackjack barked once.

"Are you two expecting someone?" Wyler said to Clayton.

Clayton had regained his composure. He glanced at Jed, whose face turned pale. Jed shook his head from side to side. Clayton grinned, then with a vacant look in his eyes, he said, "We're all dead now."

Who the hell was this? Did Gino escape? Even if he did, he couldn't have alerted people that quickly without a phone, could he? Wyler stepped into the room, picked the revolver off the floor, and shoved it in his pocket. His instincts told him something wasn't right. Wyler grabbed Jed by the back of his shirt and dragged him to his feet.

"Whoever this is, get rid of them," Wyler said.

"Fuck no," Jed said. "I don't know who that is."

"Well, you're about to find out." Wyler shoved Jed out of the room with the Glock pressed into his spine. As Wyler moved to the front door, Blackjack whined and paced. With all of Wyler's dogs, he knew to trust their signals. And the signal from Blackjack meant hell was coming.

"Guard the other room," Wyler said to Blackjack. When the dog disappeared into the room where Clayton was, Wyler took the vacated space and peeked out the window. A black SUV with the headlights off crept hauntingly up the long driveway. It wasn't a promising sign. *Friends don't drive with their headlights off.* The SUV stopped twenty yards from the house. Wyler couldn't tell how many people were inside the vehicle. No one got out. *Did the lights in the house throw them off? Were they expecting no one to be home?*

Then the four doors of the SUV opened at the same time. Four men dressed in all black filed out. Then a fifth man emerged, who Wyler recognized as Gino. Two men went left, Gino and another went right, and the fifth walked straight toward the door. It appeared to Wyler they were trying to surround the house. In the darkness, he couldn't determine whether they were armed, but he assumed they were. Thirty seconds later, a knock came at the door.

"Clayton. You in there?" the voice on the other side of the door said. "Enzo sent us out to help with the drop tonight. Open up." The man pounded on the door harder. "Clayton."

Wyler whispered into Jed's ear. "Answer him." Then he pushed Jed to his feet. Jed paused, debating refusing the order. He went to the door and said, "Who's there?"

"Jonny," the voice replied. "Who's that? Jed?"

"We don't know any Jonny. Enzo didn't tell us you were coming."

"All I know is he told us to come out and give you a hand for tonight. You gonna open the door or what?"

"We can handle the drop ourselves," Jed said. "You can tell Enzo that."

"Kid, quit fucking around and open the door."

"Call Enzo and let me hear it from him."

Silence followed then. Jed took a step closer to the door. He pressed his ear to it to see if the guy was still there. A second later, a massive boom roared as a hole the size of a cantaloupe blew through the door.

Chapter 19

Bits of wood and a shotgun slug lodged into Jed's stomach. He doubled over and dropped to the floor. Another boom rang out, decimating the door handle. The guy outside then busted his way into the house. He racked his shotgun—a pistol grip model with no stock—and lumbered inside, focused on Jed. The door partially blocked him from Wyler's view. The guy fired another round, ending what life remained in the body at his feet. He spit, turned and stepped past the door. At this point, Wyler squeezed off two shots from the Glock in quick succession. Both rounds found their mark right below the man's neck. He pitched to his left and crashed to the floor. Wyler steadied his arm and fired a single shot into the man's skull. Adrenaline surged through Wyler's veins.

Wyler rose from his position but remained low. He pushed the door shut. Then he went to the man he'd just killed. A clear earpiece dangled by the side of his bloodied face. Wyler picked it up and listened. Voices spoke in hurried Italian. He tossed the earpiece and patted the man down for any other weapons. Another Glock 19 was in a holster on the man's hip. Wyler popped the magazine and put it in his back pocket. A smash of glass came from the right. Wyler slipped the Glock in the front of his pants in an appendix-style carry. He snatched the shotgun, racked a round, and headed to where he heard the glass breaking. A short hallway opened into a kitchen. Wyler flattened himself against the wall and edged forward. Then he spun into the room, seeking a target. Off to the left, a side door was opening. Wyler fired the shotgun into the door. Someone shouted. He racked and fired again, then racked one more time, but the gun was empty. Wyler tossed it aside and retrieved the Glock.

A hail of automatic gunfire sprayed the kitchen seconds later. Wyler dove to the ground as bullets chewed through the walls above him. He army crawled back down the hallway, turned the corner, and moved to a seated position.

"Blackjack, on me," Wyler shouted. When Blackjack appeared, Wyler petted him, and said, "Shit's getting hairy, boy. Stay close to me now."

As Wyler stood, one of the hitmen rushed out of the hallway, firing his gun wildly and yelling. The gun, an HK MP5, appeared. Wyler reacted when the front of the gun swung in his direction. He released the Glock and latched both hands around the barrel of the HK. He shoved up as the hitman resumed firing. Rounds peppered the ceiling. Bits of sheetrock rained down on them. Wyler pushed his weight forward, so the hitman stumbled back off balance. When the thirty-round magazine finally emptied, Wyler stopped, planted his feet, and drove his knee into the man's stomach. Then he yanked the gun down by his side, while simultaneously ramming his forehead into the bridge of the guy's nose. The two strikes allowed Wyler to rip the weapon from his hands.

In the act of tearing the gun away, the hitman lunged at Wyler. Staggering back, they tripped over the first dead hitman. They crumpled in a heap, knocking the wind from Wyler's lungs. A second later, a fist hit him in the face. Brilliant colors flashed across Wyler's sight. He managed to get his forearms up in time to absorb the shock from another blow aimed at his head. Blood from the man's shattered nose dripped onto Wyler's face. The man was bigger, heavier than Wyler. And from how he withstood Wyler's initial hits, it was clear he had been in serious fights before.

Seeing his partner in trouble, Blackjack didn't wait for a command and joined the scrap. He bit down on the hitman's sleeve, distracting him long enough for Wyler to strike a jab into the hitman's chin. Combined with Blackjack's tugging, the man rolled off Wyler. Blackjack released the sleeve to dodge a wild kick. Pushing through the haze, Wyler rocked to his stomach, quickly pressed up to his knees, and drew the Sig from his hip. This froze the hitman in place. Before Wyler could pull the trigger, another guy—also armed with an MP5—stormed through the shattered front door. Wyler switched targets, and squeezed off two rounds, missing the newcomer by inches. The newcomer fired off shots as he retreated from the house.

The frozen-in-place hitman rushed Wyler again, but Blackjack caught him by the leg. At a five-foot distance, Wyler couldn't miss. The Sig bucked twice in his hands. Each bullet entered his attacker's chest, inches apart, dropping him dead to the floor.

"Good boy," Wyler said to Blackjack. Then he got to his feet and kicked the front door closed again. He hustled to the short hallway and swung the door open. Stairs led to a basement.

"Search," Wyler said to Blackjack. The dog ran forward and hurried down the stairs with Wyler right behind him. At the bottom, Wyler flipped down his night vision goggles. He spotted Blackjack sniffing out the damp basement. A minute later, Wyler deemed the space safe for the time being. He took a position where he had a protected yet clear firing line of anyone coming down the stairs.

As he caught his breath, he ran a mental calculation of who was left. Jed, he was pretty sure, was dead. Two of the hitmen he had personally killed. Wyler wasn't sure if he had got the guy trying to come in through the kitchen. So that left two, possibly three, guys to fend off. For ammo, he had lost the Glock but had at least eight to nine rounds left in the Sig, plus he had more 9mm in the spare Glock magazine. He popped open the cylinder of Clayton's revolver, plucked out the spent shells, and counted three remaining rounds. The amount of ammo gave him some leeway, but he needed to make every remaining shot count if he wanted to come out alive.

"Are you ok?" Wyler asked Blackjack.

Blackjack barked once. *Good.*

Wyler's head hurt like hell, but his vision had cleared at least. He inspected the basement from his position, searching for any objects or ideas to swing the odds in his favor. His eyes settled on the fuse box. He hurried over to it and killed the power to the house. If the hit team's objective was Clayton, they'd have to get inside one way or the other. Wyler considered the offhand chance they would abort the mission and leave, but he figured that was wishful thinking. Based on the hardware they carried and their skills, he took them as professionals that would try to finish the job no matter the obstacles. The two main entrance points were the kitchen and the front door. If they were smart, they'd send in a man through each entry simultaneously, knowing it would be difficult for Wyler to fend off an attack from two directions. Then a third man could trail behind for reinforcements.

Wyler's stomach sank as he thought of reinforcements. *Would they call in more people? How badly did they want Clayton dead?* He reasoned out what he knew. The time the crew arrived led Wyler to assume they weren't expecting Clayton and Jed to be home. Or if they did, they certainly didn't plan on resistance. If that was the case, getting more people out to the house bought Wyler time. Their location gave him forty-five minutes to an hour. He needed to go on the offensive.

He paced the back wall until he found the door leading to the outside. Opening it revealed eight stairs leading to a sloped metal double door. Wyler pushed gently on one of the doors with his left hand. Through the small crack he created, he surveyed the area, then he lowered it back into place.

Wyler whispered to Blackjack. "We're going to have to go quick coming out of here. Don't stop moving." He scratched Blackjack's head. "Stay safe."

Blackjack accepted the affection but remained at attention, ready to work.

Wyler gripped the Sig in his right hand and pressed the metal door open.

"Search," Wyler said.

Blackjack sprinted up the stairs and into the night. He made it two yards before gunfire broke the silence of the air. Blackjack serpentined away from the hail of bullets, changing his path for the cover of the nearest treeline. Climbing to the last step, Wyler popped over the top of the door, using it as a partial shield. The muzzle flash from the machine gun stood out like the sun against the blackness of the night. Wyler pointed the Sig two inches above the flash and fired until it vanished.

He darted out from the stairwell, making a hundred-and-eighty-degree sweep with the pistol. No other shots came, so he ran to the motionless lump on the ground. The gunman lay on his side, dead. At least one of the bullets had caught the man in the throat. *Another one down. One to two threats left.* Wyler holstered the Sig and then pushed the dead guy over. He picked up the machine gun and quickly extracted the magazine. Seeing a few rounds still inside, he reinserted it.

Breaking glass sounded behind him. He spun as a beam from a flashlight frantically probed the darkness to locate the source of the gunfire. Wyler nestled the MP5 stock into his shoulder and unleashed a three-round burst into the window as the light found him. A strained shout followed. Then the flashlight disappeared into the room. Wyler watched the spot for a few seconds as the glow from the flashlight didn't seem to move. He hoped that was another threat out of commission. That left him either one or possibly no one left. Wyler sprinted to the right side of the house to capitalize on the momentum and confusion. He tossed aside the machine gun, not wanting to risk it running out of bullets when he needed it. Drawing the Sig, he crept to the edge of the house and peered into the front yard. Someone had turned on the headlights of the SUV. To give them some visibility going into the house, he guessed. The intensity of the lights forced Wyler to switch off his night vision. The driver-side door hung open. Wyler couldn't discern any shapes of a person inside the vehicle. He decided to clear it before attempting a final push back into the house.

After a check behind him, he edged out into the yard, sidestepping parallel to the SUV. His gun pressed forward, sweeping his field of view. When he came even with the open door, he inspected the interior from a distance. Seeing nothing, he advanced to the door—his senses working on overdrive. *How many people were left? Was the SUV a decoy or some kind of...*

Glass erupted from the driver's window. Shards peppered the side of Wyler's face. A burst of sharp pain flooded his nervous system. *Ignore it;* his survival instinct screamed at him. *Move.* Another boom, followed by the windshield splintering into an intricate weaving of hairline cracks. Wyler dove into the front seat, keeping his torso beneath the dash for protection. One more round came through the windshield, exploding into the seat inches above his head.

In a split second, Wyler wrenched down on the shifter, throwing the vehicle into drive. He reached down and shoved his palm onto the accelerator. The big Cadillac spun its tires on the dirt before catching and launching forward. The ground was level, allowing the vehicle to gain some speed. Another round pumped through the windshield, destroying the remnants of its integrity and sending a wave of glass everywhere. Wyler popped his head over the dash. The twenty-yard distance closed quickly. He ducked his head, pressed harder on the gas for another two seconds, released it, and braced for impact.

Airbags burst from their compartments as the Cadillac bulldozed through the front of the house. They did their job keeping Wyler alive, but his awkward position in the seat left him with at least a bruised rib. The Cadillac came to a violent stop, half inside, half outside the house's threshold. *Don't stop,* the voice in his head yelled. *Move.* Wyler spilled out of the SUV, landing on his knees, then rolled to a seated position. The Sig was nowhere to be found. *Not good.* His eyes darted around the room for the shooter amongst the debris and dust. *Had he hit them?* A crunching sound came from near the hood of the Cadillac. Someone stepping through the litter of 2x4s and sheetrock. He needed a weapon. *Find something. Anything.* Then he remembered the revolver in his pocket.

Right as his fingers looped around the wood handle of the gun, a guy jumped into view. From the glow of light coming from the SUV, Wyler saw the guy was holding a shotgun.

"Look how the tides turned, mother fucker," the guy said. As he took a step closer, Wyler recognized Gino. "I'm going to savor watching you bleed the fuck out, you piece of shit." Gino glanced down to get his footing on the cluttered floor. As he did, Wyler used the opportunity to slide his hand with the revolver out of his pocket.

"A nice little gut shot ought to do the trick," Gino said, aiming loosely toward Wyler's stomach. *Keep talking. One step closer.* Enough of Wyler was shrouded in shadows that he didn't think Gino could see the revolver. *Steady your breathing. Slow your heart down. Mess this up and it's over.* Wyler held his wrist on the ground but tilted the gun roughly where he thought it aligned with Gino. Any hit would do.

Gino started to say, "Anything you want to..." But the concussion of the revolver firing cut him off. The longer, harder pull of the double-action trigger caused Wyler's shot to go higher and more to the right than he wanted. The bullet missed. Gino flinched from surprise and panic-pulled the trigger of the shotgun. An empty click. Out of bullets. Wyler raised the revolver and fired. This time the .38 round entered near Gino's collarbone. The shotgun tumbled from Gino's hands as he clutched a spot below his neck. Gino sank to the floor, gurgling as he choked on his blood.

Using the Cadillac door, Wyler hoisted himself to his feet. He stepped through the mess until he stood over Gino's twitching body. Wyler cocked the hammer with his thumb, squared the sights on Gino's face, and fired the remaining bullet, ending a prolonged death. Before Wyler relaxed, he needed to account for everyone. He tallied seven people on the property. In the room where he currently stood, he counted four bodies. Gino, Jed, and two of the four hitmen. The one outside the basement was another. That left the shooter from the window and Clayton.

Once Wyler traversed the carnage the Cadillac created, he shuffled into the hallway where he had stashed Clayton. For the moment, he bypassed the door and moved to the end of the hall. In the bathroom, lying on the tile floor, was another hitman. Wyler eased next to him and picked up his MP5. With the barrel resting on the man's chest, Wyler checked for a pulse. Nothing. *Six down. Clayton's it.* Backtracking, Wyler entered the room where he last saw his original target.

In the far corner, Clayton sat on the ground. His still taped wrists were cupped against his stomach. Blood saturated his shirt down into his pants. Wyler glanced over his shoulder. A trail of bullet holes decorated the wall. *A stray one must have got him.* Wyler crouched a foot away from Clayton. Sweat covered his pale pained face. His chest heaved as he labored for breath. From the amount of blood and the color of it, Wyler knew Clayton didn't have much longer to live. He'd seen more people die from gut shots than he cared to remember. They all had that same dazed and distant look in their eyes as if they were hovering in a different plane of reality before crossing over to the other side. It was an experience Wyler hoped to never find himself in.

"Jed?" Clayton asked after he caught some air.

Wyler shook his head. Clayton grunted as he glanced at the thick dark liquid covering his hands.

"I'm dying." He stated more than asked.

Wyler nodded.

"About how...I thought it was...going to end."

"You were doing this because of your father?" Wyler said.

Clayton ground his teeth, his face clenched in a spasm of pain. When the spasm passed he nodded his head to the question.

"He owed money to the mob?" Wyler said, recalling his conversation with Duncan, the former State Trooper.

Clayton nodded. "Killed himself...to try and get out of it...but they wouldn't...let it go..."

"They transferred the debt to you."

Clayton nodded again. "I laundered dirty money...for them... through the race track...to pay it off..."

"But then the laws passed," Wyler said. "Putting greyhound tracks out of business. And then you had to work it off? So you used dogs as drug mules. Was it to avoid crossing state lines? Avoid federal charges if you got caught? Was that the idea?"

Clayton didn't answer. A trickle of blood wound its way from his mouth. His eyes blinked as if unable to focus anymore. "Those dogs...I always hated them...ruined my life...now they..."

He murmured something Wyler couldn't understand. Clayton's eyes rolled, and then his head went slack. Wyler stared at him for a moment before checking for a pulse. None existed. Using the machine gun for support, Wyler rose and stumbled into the hallway. He navigated his way to the kitchen and exited through the side door. With the immediate threats gone, his senses came down from their heightened state. He assessed his own injuries, dabbing a finger against his face. None of the cuts from the glass were too deep. His head hurt like hell, as did some of his ribs. Nothing some rest and pain killers couldn't fix.

He turned left, heading for the backyard. "Blackjack," he shouted. Then he whistled. "On me." Wyler rounded the corner, expecting to see his canine partner bounding towards him, and when he didn't, panic squeezed his gut like a car compactor. "Blackjack. On me," he shouted again. He flipped down his night vision goggles and jogged toward the treeline opposite the basement door. "Blackjack. Where are you, boy?"

A noise came from his left. A whimper. Wyler sprinted to the location. He found Blackjack lying behind a tree. His tail wagged at the sight of Wyler.

"Jesus," Wyler said. *Don't panic.* "What happened?" Wyler eased his hand under Blackjack's head and petted him. "Where does it hurt?"

With some effort, Blackjack propped himself up and curled in. His nose nuzzled an area on his rear right leg. The goggles made it difficult for Wyler to fully assess what had happened. "Stay with me, boy. I'm going to get you out of here." He slung the MP5 over his shoulder so it dangled down his back. Then he crouched and scooped his friend into his arms. "You're going to be ok," Wyler said, trying to reassure himself more than the dog. He took off running with Blackjack's life seeping through his hands.

Chapter 20

Wyler streaked across the road and into the woods opposite Clayton's property. He stopped to flip down his night vision goggles and check his watch to get his bearings to find the Bronco. When he had the direction locked in his mind, he continued. Carrying the eighty-pound dog made his trek harder, but he didn't care. He blocked out the exhaustion and pain. Blackjack had to live. Wyler wouldn't entertain any other outcome. His legs burned. His arms ached. His head throbbed. None of it mattered as he pushed his body to the limit. Wyler tripped over a stump, and lurched to the side, crashing into a tree, but managed to remain upright. Blackjack whimpered from being jostled.

"I'm sorry, boy. Hang in there."

Fifteen minutes later, he found the Bronco.

Wyler fumbled with the keys to get it unlocked. He swung down the back gate and rested Blackjack inside. Then he ran to the front and started the vehicle. With the lights on inside, he inspected Blackjack's injuries. The hind leg had an apparent bullet wound through the thin flesh toward his paw. Wyler dug out his first aid kit. He poured a disinfectant into the hole, then wrapped it tightly in gauze. His fingers then slowly worked through Blackjack's fur, starting at his head, searching for other serious issues. Everything felt intact until he reached his upper thigh. Blood coated the fur. Something was there, but Wyler couldn't see enough to tell if a bullet had gone in or just grazed him. Wyler dumped more disinfectant on the spot and wrapped it with gauze too. He pulled out his water bottle and poured it for Blackjack to drink. Wyler wished he could do more. It would have to suffice for what he had to work with. He at least had Blackjack stabilized and slowed the bleeding. Wyler hoped it would keep him alive until he could get him proper help.

He settled Blackjack into a comfortable position and draped a blanket over him. After closing the back, he hopped into the driver's seat. Painfully, he peeled off the ski mask, feeling bits of glass still embedded in his skin. When he removed it, he chucked it on the floor, shifted into gear, and lurched the Bronco forward. As he drove, he wrangled his phone from his pocket and dialed a number.

"Come on, answer," Wyler said as the ringtone continued. After what seemed like an eternity, the line finally clicked over.

"Hello," answered the groggy voice of Hudson.

"Hudson, listen, this is Ethan. I'm in a situation here, and I need to know if you can help me with no questions asked?"

A long pause followed. Then Hudson said, "What's happened?"

"My dog has sustained two bullet wounds. One in his upper thigh and one lower down on his hind leg. I'm about thirty-five to forty minutes away from you. I can pay whatever you need."

Another long pause. "Meet me at the hospital. I can take it from there."

"I owe you."

"I'll be waiting out back."

Wyler ended the call and then tossed the phone into the passenger seat. The passenger seat normally occupied by Blackjack. His friend and partner he'd let get hurt on his watch. As he stared into the endless night, he remembered how the dog came into his life. A batch of Belgian Malinois puppies was stolen from a farm raising the dogs for a life in the military. Like the job he was working now, Arlo had convinced Wyler to help him. And he did. It took Wyler three days to find the people responsible—two heroin addicts wanting to sell the dogs to fund their drug habit. When Wyler found them, a fight ensued, leaving the two men dead. It was the first time Wyler had killed someone as a civilian.

Taking out terrorists on foreign soil for his country was one thing, but what he did to those addicts felt different. In the Marines, he had seen atrocities happening, but if the top brass told him not to engage, then that was that. He had to helplessly sit by and be a witness. On his own, though, he could act on what he thought was right. Not having to answer to anyone but himself for his actions was both terrifying and liberating at the same time.

Arlo called in favors to clean the whole mess up with the dead bodies and kept Wyler a free man. And as a show of thanks, the dog breeder gifted Blackjack to Wyler. They hadn't spent a day apart since.

Wyler gripped the wheel and stomped on the accelerator. Plenty of time to feel guilty later, he told himself. *Focus on saving your friend.* He swung the Bronco onto the highway, then opened up the retooled engine, pushing the needle over ninety. His eyes constantly scanned ahead for any signs of cops. Getting pulled over would create a lot of questions and time lost. He exited the highway. The time of night removed the bulk of traffic, allowing Wyler to make good time through the two-lane roads.

"We're almost there," Wyler yelled to Blackjack. "Stay with me."

Five minutes later, Wyler screeched to a halt in the backlot of the animal hospital. As he jumped out, he spotted Hudson standing at the door, holding it open. Wyler flung the rear gate of the Bronco down and cradled Blackjack in his arms. He placed his hand on the dog's chest and still felt movement as he hustled past Hudson into the hospital. It took him a minute for his eyes to adjust to the bright fluorescent bulbs. Hudson checked the lot for anyone around before slamming the door.

"This way," Hudson said, striding down the hall. He turned into an operating room. "Put him on the table."

Wyler followed the instruction, then stepped to the side.

"I'm going to shave a patch on his front leg, so I can get an IV going and give him something for the pain," Hudson said. "Hold him while I do it. Try and keep him calm."

Hudson grabbed an electric shear and shaved away a patch of fur. Then he cleaned the spot and inserted the needle.

"Ok, good. I'll sedate him now, then I can get to work."

"It's going to be alright," Wyler said to Blackjack, petting his head.

"Do you need to be looked at?" Hudson said, nodding at Wyler's glass-riddled face.

Wyler touched the cuts and said, "No. I'm fine. I'll deal with it later."

"I know you said to not ask questions, but do I need to worry about being an accessory to something?"

"Do you know where I was tonight?"

"No."

"Then you'll be fine. If, on the offhand chance, the cops should ask questions, tell them what you want. You don't need to get caught up in anything because of me."

Hudson nodded.

Then, remembering the greyhounds, Wyler said, "I've got some things that need finishing."

"You're leaving?"

"I'll be back as soon as possible," Wyler said. "If something...if something should happen, text me. Please do whatever you can to keep him alive. Whatever it costs, you'll get it."

"He's in good hands," Hudson said with determined reassurance.

"Thank you," Wyler said, extending his hand. Hudson shook it. Wyler took one last look at Blackjack, leaving the room, determined to make his sacrifice worth something.

After leaving the animal hospital, Wyler drove to the hotel. In his room, he stripped off his blood-soaked shirt and tossed it in the waste paper basket. He went into the bathroom and studied his face in the mirror. With his knife, he dug out the pieces of glass embedded in his skin. Then he poured disinfectant over the cuts. Wyler gritted his teeth from the sharp sting of the liquid. When the sensation subsided, he washed his face with cold water, which brought him back to life. He threw on a fresh shirt and then packed the few items he had left in the room. His time was up in this location, despite whatever happened in the next few hours.

When the cops eventually showed up at Clayton's property,

Wyler didn't want to hang around for them to come asking him questions. He would get the greyhounds to safety, collect Blackjack, and then head home to Atlantic City to pick up where he had left off. Wyler replayed the last few days in his mind to assess his potential exposure. Hudson knew him by his fake name, so he was covered there. But Hudson did know Wyler was interested in the greyhound and where the dog was found. Hudson helped mend bullet wounds in Wyler's dog, but he didn't know how it happened. Wyler was on Sid's cameras which could create a problem. He made a mental note to enlist Mack's services one last time to erase the footage. Otherwise, the people he came in contact with were either dead, didn't know his real name, or were involved with crimes themselves bringing him the security of mutually assured destruction. Forensics might be able to lift his prints and possibly some of his blood from Clayton's, but he banked on that being a stretch of proving anything.

He had some potential holes if questioned but had enough vagueness in his actions that wouldn't lead to an arrest. If his name did happen to get mentioned in any police investigations, then it was up to Arlo and his connections to run interference and keep Wyler clean. He did a final pass over the room. Satisfied he left nothing behind, Wyler tied off the plastic waste paper bag containing his bloodied shirt, grabbed his gear, and left the room. At the front desk, he dropped off the key card and checked out with the overnight desk clerk.

In the Bronco, Wyler made a quick stop at a late-night convenience store. In their Dumpster, he tossed the bag with his bloody clothes. Then he went inside, paying cash for a cup of coffee, a gallon of water, and a bottle of painkillers. With the water, he washed down four pills and then sipped on the coffee. As the pills and coffee went to work, giving his body a jolt, he input the coordinates to Clayton's house and set off to finish what he had started.

The forty-minute drive was agony for Wyler. Too much time for his mind to wander. *Were the lives of thirty greyhounds worth the life of Blackjack's? Why had he agreed to this? He should have stayed in New Jersey. Or was he selfish thinking that? What did he stand for? At his core, he wanted to protect life no matter its form and dole out justice to those who didn't respect it.* A different part of his mind chimed in. *Focus. Get the job done. You agreed to the job. Now see it through. Do it for Blackjack. Do it for Thunder. Do it for Reno. Do it for yourself.*

He rolled down his windows and turned on some music, cranking it to a blaring level to drown out his conflicting thoughts. It helped. Forty minutes later, Wyler approached Clayton's property by the main road. He killed the music and slowed down. Something caught his eye, and he immediately switched off the lights of the Bronco, braked, and pulled off the road. He reached into the back and found his night vision monocular. Putting it to his eye, he zoomed in. Three other big SUVs were parked in front of Clayton's house. A handful of people worked the scene. Two men carried a dead body and loaded it into the back of one of the SUVs. Others held the used weapons from the hitmen in their arms. They lacked any identifying wardrobe of cops or federal agents.

"Fuck," Wyler said, lowering the monocular. *Scrubbing the place clean. Erasing everything that happened.* Wyler looked through the device again. At the shed, two men loaded the greyhounds into the trailer attached to Clayton's truck. Finishing the job just got more complicated.

Chapter 21

Two hours prior, Enzo Crippa was awoken by a pinging of his phone. He didn't recognize the number and let the call go to voicemail. A moment later, Enzo put the phone to his ear and listened to the message.

Gino's amped-up voice came through. "Boss. It's me, G. Someone jumped me and is going to our man's house. I'm with the other crew you sent out here. I'm calling from one of their phones. I'll let you know what's happening when we get there."

The call ended. Unsettled by the message, Enzo got out of bed and went to his bathroom. After a quick shower, he got dressed and waited for the update from Gino. He went down to the kitchen to not disturb his wife. *What the hell was happening? Was it this lone prick again causing issues? Who was this guy? Someone from a rival gang? But who? Who would start a possible war over a small operation? Or was it some random guy who'd watched too many vigilante movies? Either way, he was becoming a problem that needed to disappear quickly.*

The coffee finished brewing, and Enzo was halfway through a cup when his phone buzzed again. He recognized Gino's voice, but this time it conveyed pure panic.

"Boss. Shits gone south. The crew has been taken out. Send as many men as you can. Hurry. I don't know how much longer I can hold out. Boss..."

His voice broke off then, and a thump came through the line as if he'd dropped the phone. Then loud bursts of gunfire echoed, causing Enzo to pull it away from his ear.

"Gino?" Enzo said. "Gino. Are you there?"

More chaotic sounds reverberated, then the line went dead.

"Gino," he shouted. "Son of a bitch."

Enraged and confused, Enzo considered who had the means to dispatch a crew of four as experienced as Lucian's. Things turned serious for Enzo at that moment. Keeping the peace with the Bama Boys was one thing, but if word got out Lucian was off the market because of a job Enzo ordered—he shuddered to think of what would come next. *Who would seek him out for revenge? How many other gangs that used his services would hold him responsible for taking a major talent off the board? Then there was Nico. How would he take the embarrassment?* Panic crept up Enzo's spine. The perfect world he'd built over decades suddenly was at risk of collapsing, burying him in a shallow grave.

He needed to act with urgency to right the ship before he totally lost control. After taking a breath, Enzo called one of his trusted lieutenants, Rocco.

"Boss?" answered the drowsy voice after six rings. "It's late. Everything good?"

"No, Rocco, I'm not good. I need you to gather up as many

guys as you can and come pick me up as soon as possible. Make sure they're equipped, and bring supplies for a cleaning job, you know what I mean?"

"Fuck. What's going on?"

"A problem we need to make seem like it never happened."

"Who's involved?"

"Just get the fuck over here. I'll give you the details on the way."

Enzo mashed his finger into the red button ending the call. He thought for a moment, then rang Bruno, who maintained the three boats the Toro family used for various jobs. In this case, Enzo needed them for unloading bodies. When Bruno answered, Enzo said, "I need you up right now and get one of the boats fueled. A few packages are coming tonight that need a new home."

"Jesus, Enzo, do you know what time it is?"

"Yeah, I know what time it is, and if you want to live to see the morning, you'll shut the fuck up and do what you're told."

Enzo ended the call with the same gusto. With the wheels in motion, he went to his closet and opened a safe concealed in the floor. He pulled out a serial number free handgun and tucked it into his pants. Then he went outside and waited for Rocco. His black SUV arrived forty minutes later. Two more SUVs pulled up behind him.

"What the fuck took you so long?" Enzo snarled as he got into the back seat.

"Sorry, boss. It's late. It took me a bit to track everyone down and get them going."

"Fine. Whatever. Drive."

"Where am I going?"

"Clayton Judge's place."

"You got an address?"

Enzo found it in his phone and showed it to another guy from his crew in the passenger seat.

"Let's make it fast," Enzo said.

Once they were driving, Rocco said, "What's at this guy, Judge's place?"

A mess that can be a death sentence.

"Just fucking drive," Enzo said.

Enzo realized the thoughts were an understatement as he climbed the debris into Clayton's living room. With the power turned back on, the lights revealed two dead bodies to the left of the Cadillac lodged in the doorway. He recognized Gino, and the other, based on his attire, he placed as part of Lucian's team. In front of the big SUV was another body, another of Lucian's men. As Enzo came to the right side of the vehicle, he spotted Jed, or at least who he thought was Jed. The better part of his face was a mangled mess of flesh and bone from the impact of a close-range shotgun slug. The sight made something unpleasant stir in Enzo's stomach.

"Boss," Rocco shouted from down the hallway. "We got more down here."

Enzo walked over to him. "Where?"

Rocco pointed into the second room, where Clayton sat dead on the ground, his wrists still bound. Enzo crouched in front of the body, looking it over. A sizable blood stain lined Clayton's shirt near his stomach. Using a clean piece of clothes from the floor, Enzo wrapped his hand, placed it under Clayton's chin, and lifted the man's head. *At least the night wasn't a total loss.*

"Where's the other one?" Enzo asked, standing.

"In the bathroom, on the right," Rocco said.

A similar scene was on display in the bathroom. Another of

Lucian's men was dead from at least two bullet wounds.

"Who do you think did this, boss?"

"I've got some ideas," Enzo said, despite having little understanding of who was responsible for the destruction in front of him. He struggled to accept the possibility of one man doing this amount of damage. The heavy stench of death filled his lungs. He needed air. Walking down the hallway, Enzo then turned down the corridor to the kitchen. His expensive shoes crunched over the shattered glass as he exited through the side door.

"What do you want to do?" Rocco asked, following Enzo outside.

Enzo considered his options, then said, "How many men do we have here?"

"Aside from me and you, ten."

"Alright, this is what I want you to do in this order. Wrap up the bodies, and load them into one of the Caddies. Send two guys you trust to handle themselves down to the docks. I told Bruno to expect someone with a package tonight. Have them dump all the bodies."

"Ok."

"Then collect any weapons you can find, and toss them in the pond over there. While that's happening, have another one of your men get the Cadillac out of the house. Have them take it somewhere discreet. Strip the plates, then burn the vehicle."

Enzo noticed the shed a few yards away. He walked towards it with Rocco in tow. When he got to the doors, Enzo said, "Open it."

Rocco did, and then he stepped inside and searched the wall until he found a light switch.

"Fucking stinks in here," Rocco said, putting the back of his hand to his nose in a useless attempt to block the smell. Enzo stepped in and studied the crates of dogs. If he finished what Clayton started, and got the batch of dogs with the drugs to the Bama Boys, then that would take care of them. They got their drugs, and Clayton was dead. He could downplay the specifics to Nico, keeping the information vague and high level. *Drugs delivered, and Clayton gone.* That was all Nico had asked of him. Enzo would float his men a little extra cash to stick to the same story. Then if he succeeded in making Lucian and his men disappear, Enzo rationalized he could come out from this disaster somewhat unscathed.

"Load these dogs up," Enzo said.

"Which ones?"

Enzo didn't know which dogs had the drugs in them. He couldn't take a chance sending the wrong ones, so he said, "Load all of them. Use their truck. I'll give you the number of someone with the Bama Boys. They're going to tell you a spot to drive these dogs. You do what they say. These guys used an ATV to run the dogs to the Bama Boys through a clearing. Think you can handle that?"

"If these dipshits did it, I'm sure we can figure it out."

"Once they've got the dogs, ditch the truck, and you can consider your job done for the night."

"What do the Bama Boys want with some dogs?"

"Don't worry about that. This is important, though. I'm trusting you to take care of this personally. If they don't get these dogs, all of us will have a problem. Understand?"

"No, not really, boss, but I don't have to. I'll take care of it. You can count on me."

"Good," Enzo said and tapped away on his phone. "I texted you the number to call. When it's done, let me know. After we get this cleaned up, we can figure out who to fuck up for messing with us."

Rocco grinned. "Sounds good, boss."

"And Rocco..."

"Yeah?"

"Make sure your men understand what happened here isn't meant to be broadcast to the world. If I hear about someone running their mouth, they'll have to answer to me. And I can guarantee you, they won't be happy about it."

"I'll let them know," Rocco said. "You should get out of here now, in case the cops show up or whoever did this comes back."

"I've sounded like a broken record lately, but no fuck ups on this. Far too many have already happened."

"We'll handle it."

"I'll have my phone on me, and I'll be up the rest of the night. Call me for anything."

"You got it."

Rocco turned and went back into the house. Enzo collected a bodyguard to drive him home. As the Cadillac reversed, Enzo shook his head in disgust. He hated sloppiness, and the scene he stared at epitomized the sentiment. *Clayton and his idea showed promise, but sometimes that just wasn't enough.*

Chapter 22

Wyler studied the scene unfolding. Two men got into one of the vehicles. They were leaving. The location was too deserted for him to remain parked where he was. He couldn't risk them spotting him. After tossing the monocular onto the passenger seat, he slammed the Bronco into reverse, speeding away until he lost sight of the property. He cut the wheel as he braked, throwing the vehicle into a turn. With practiced precision, he shifted into drive, flipped on his lights, and rode the truck's horsepower. Wyler swung the Bronco onto the next available dirt path cutting through the woods. He killed the lights again when he was far enough out of sight. His eyes flicked back and forth between the rearview mirror and his phone. He called up his map and scanned it for the nearest side road to stake out the remainder of the cleanup operation at Clayton's.

Once he found an ideal spot, he waited two minutes longer to watch for any passing headlights of the vehicle leaving. Not seeing any, he drove on. The new location was farther to the east than his original hideaway but kept him concealed. He counted at least ten or eleven men. Too many for him to attempt a head-on assault on his own. Even if Blackjack was with him, the odds weren't there. Two men stood by the shed discussing something. Then they opened the trailer attached to Clayton's truck, checking out the inside of it. After a brief conversation, they returned to the shed. A few minutes later, they began transporting the greyhounds to the trailer. Wyler counted each one as they went. It took the men over half an hour to load all the dogs. Thirty in total, Wyler calculated.

His attention shifted to one of the other SUVs. Four of the men carried large objects that looked like rolled carpets. They stuffed the rolls into the trunk. Throughout four trips, they loaded in seven of them. Getting rid of the bodies, Wyler figured. Whoever these people were, they worked efficiently and with a good deal of organization—something they'd done before. The seventh body required three men to shove it on top of the pile. When they finished, two men got in and drove off.

A group focused on the Cadillac Wyler had driven into the living room. Twenty minutes passed before they freed it. One guy hopped in the passenger seat, and the busted Cadillac limped away. Three of the remaining men disappeared into the house while the others congregated near the shed.

Wyler took the brief downtime to grab the MP5 he'd brought. He ejected the magazine and counted the remaining rounds—eighteen. Not the ideal number of bullets to take on the seven men left at the property. About two rounds per man. Wyler considered his knife and knuckledusters in his weapons inventory, but that required close quarters. The idea of trying to snipe a few men with the MP5 crossed his mind only for an instant. It wasn't practical. His marksmanship skills were solid, but from the range he was at, how many could he hope to get? Two guys at the most? That still left five. His situation would remain the same in that scenario, and his chances of rescuing the dogs would plummet. No, he thought, this night was turning into a trail and stalk strategy. *Watch and wait for the opportune time to strike. Patience.*

A soft glow of light grabbed his attention. He returned to the monocular as three men sprinted from the house. The glow increased. They had set the house on fire. A simple solution to destroy evidence and make it harder for future investigators to understand what had happened. With the house blaze spreading, four men climbed into the SUV, and another three piled into Clayton's truck with the dogs. Clayton's truck led the way off the property, turning left at the end of the driveway. The SUV went after it. Wyler counted to ten, then drove out of his hiding spot, ready to track his prey.

Wyler hung back a reasonable distance with his headlights off. He occasionally sped up until he could see the SUV to make sure he still had them, then he would drop back. The area was too desolate, and too late at night for him to trail them closely without making them suspicious. If the men had taken the dogs, Wyler assumed they planned to deliver them to Sid and his people like before. He had two ways to play things. The first was to try and overtake both vehicles. The SUV, he could shoot out one of the front tires by driving alongside them and emptying the MP5. Then he would have to try and get Clayton's truck to stop without a crash, which could hurt or kill the greyhounds, which defeated the purpose. Without a good solution for stopping Clayton's truck, he shifted his thinking to how he could overtake them at the dropoff site. They would be stationary, at least, giving him a better chance to contain an escape.

His mind suddenly snapped into the present. He sat straighter behind the wheel as his heartbeat quickened, seeing a fork in the road ahead.

"Shit," he said, mashing his foot into the pedal. The Bronco's electric engine whirred. He'd let them get too far ahead of him. *Stupid. Stupid. Stupid.* He was thinking of too many things at once. Blackjack getting shot left him rattled, distracted. *Get it together. Focus. Don't let Blackjack getting shot be for nothing.* You've come too far to mess things up now. When he got to the junction, Wyler studied the two directions he could take for a few seconds each. *Which way would they have gone?* The longer he waited, the more distance the dogs got from him. He went with his gut and turned left. Throwing caution to the wind, he flipped on his low beams to close ground faster. One mile down. Still not seeing them, his heart raced as quickly as the engine. *Had he gone the wrong way? Had he lost them completely? Stupid. He shouldn't have let them create that much distance.* He pushed the Bronco harder. Then he spotted a speck of red in the distance. Taillights. Wyler needed to confirm it was his target, though. To get close enough, he would have to drive past them so they didn't think he was following them. He accelerated gradually, building a natural speed to overtake the two-vehicle convoy. But as he got closer, he sensed something was wrong.

"Fuck," Wyler said as he banged his fist on the steering wheel and braked hard.

Clayton's truck wasn't in front of the SUV. The two vehicles must have parted ways at the fork. Wyler swore at himself again.

He had picked the wrong direction.

After a quick k-turn, Wyler sped back down the road he came from. Angry at his mistake, he fired up the screen on the Bronco's dash and pulled up a map. His eyes glanced at it, then the road repeatedly, attempting to figure out where Clayton's truck went. Luckily for him, they were still mainly in a rural area, so the options were limited. He thought of something then. Sid's cameras. He extracted his phone from his jeans and tapped the screen, careful not to careen off the road. After a few seconds, he pulled up the app and studied the footage.

"Damn it," he said, not seeing anyone in the clearing the cameras watched. His thoughts spiraled. *Had the plans to drop off the dogs been scrapped because of everything that had happened? Whoever these guys were, did they intend to keep the dogs and drugs for themselves? Or were they still dropping them off but at a different location?* If they were still going to Sid at the Klempt property, he had a chance. If they were going somewhere entirely different, then he didn't have a shot in hell of finding them before the dogs were executed. He would have failed them. Failed Blackjack. Failed Arlo. Failed himself.

Wyler pulled off to the side of the road and stopped. He took a deep breath, centering his mind. *Focus,* he told himself. He pinched on the screen, zooming out. Then he panned to get his bearings. The route he was currently on headed toward the general direction of the Klempts and their murder barn. He convinced himself the dogs were still headed there. Accepting anything less was accepting his failure. He analyzed the map and plotted the most logical way to reach the borderline. *They want to avoid crossing state lines. There are only so many places they can go to get the drugs to the other side.* He picked a road to follow and drove. If he couldn't find them, he could, at the bare minimum, return to the Klempts and attempt a last-ditch effort there. The more time Wyler spent driving with no view of the truck, the more his chest tightened with the hard truth he had blown it.

Chapter 23

A mile into his frantic chase, Wyler had one last-ditch idea. He picked up the burner phone, getting Mack on the line.

"I might be able to retire off of this operation of yours by the time you're done," Mack said.

"There's a good chance of that."

"What do you need now?"

"I need to find somebody driving in real-time. Maybe within ten to fifteen miles of my current location. And I needed to find them about ten minutes ago."

Mack laughed. "So nothing big?"

"Got any ideas?"

Mack went quiet for a few beats. "Yeah, I've got a way to do it, but I'm not sure how quick it can be done. What's your realistic time window?"

"Maybe thirty minutes tops."

"Give me a second to pull up your location from your phone."

The tapping of keys sounded like a firing squad executing seconds.

"Alright, I've got you," Mack said. "Now, let me do some calculations."

"What're you thinking?"

"How'd we do it overseas?"

"Drones?"

"Ding," Mack said. "Luckily for you, drones have seen a big uptick in the commercial market over the past few years. I've used a bunch of guys for some past surveillance jobs. That'll be your best bet. But it's a matter of how fast one of them can get to you. It wouldn't have been an issue if there was advanced notice."

"Do what you can."

"I'll get back to you. Hang tight."

The line went dead. Wyler focused on the road ahead, clinging to the long-shot odds. His belief in luck was one he learned from his father. The belief saw luck as an empty token. The way it was filled was correlated over a span of time where things didn't break a person's way. Something like losing a month's paycheck on one spin of roulette to only have your number hit on the next spin. The longer the dry spell, the more the token filled. Once it hit capacity, the odds increased exponentially for a lucky break to occur. If one happened before it was filled, the token was reset to zero. The minutiae of the belief left a lot to be desired, but at the moment, it was all Wyler had.

The burner phone buzzed ten minutes later. Wyler answered on the second ring.

"What have you got?"

"Drones in the air now. It will be close timing-wise, but you've got a chance. What are we looking for?"

Wyler exhaled. "A white Chevy Silverado, maybe around a 2010 model. A large black trailer attached to the back end."

"Good. Anything else you can think of to help narrow the search?"

"They've got maybe a ten-minute headstart on me. Look up Mason Klempt of Alabama. From his property, pull a twenty-mile radius toward my current location. I'd grid that section."

"Understood. Stay on the line. I'll guide you in if we find it."

"Ok." Wyler attached the phone to a holder above the dash and waited for Lady Luck's verdict. He kept his speed in the mid-40s, not wanting to create too much separation in case he had to double back again. The clock on the control console ticked away. One minute turned into five, and then five turned into ten. At the twenty-minute mark, Wyler glared at the clock, willing it to slow down. Still no sign of the truck.

Mack spoke then. "Ok. The drone is coming into range. Commencing sweep now."

Wyler leaned forward, readjusting his grip on the steering wheel. Another minute passed, and then another. He wiped the sweat dripping into his eyes. *They had to be close.* Another minute ticked by.

"Hold on," Mack said. "We've got movement. Get closer." The silence was maddening to Wyler.

"White Chevy truck with a black trailer attached, heading northwest. Two miles away. We've got them."

"Where am I going?"

"You're south and heading away from them. Go straight for another mile. Take the first left."

"Got it."

Wyler stomped the pedal. The Bronco whipped forward until

the left-hand turn materialized. He decelerated enough to take the turn without flipping the vehicle.

"Where now?"

"You're on this for another two miles. You'll come to a slight fork. Stay left."

The speedometer inched up to ninety. *You're almost there. You can still save them. Move.* Wyler got to the fork and gunned it, hurtling over the pavement.

"Good," Mack said. "One mile on this, then a right turn, and then you're on them. At your current speed, you should see them in less than five minutes."

"Mack, if I knew your real name, I'd name my firstborn after you."

Mack chuckled. "Happy hunting."

The call ended. Wyler tightened his grip as the Bronco made short work of the last mile. He banked to the right, then slowed down, scanning for the truck. A half mile away, the white of reversing tail lights cut through the curtain of night.

There you are. He flipped off his lights and pulled off the road. *If the truck was reversing, they must not have been able to find the turn-off spot for the new drop site.* He grabbed the monocular and locked in on the truck. It reversed slowly a little further, then idled. After a brief pause, it disappeared into the trees. Wyler approached cautiously where he saw them go. He squinted into the entrance before going any farther. *Don't rush it now.* He put on his night vision goggles and placed the MP5 next to him on the seat. With his lights off, and the goggles on, he proceeded into the narrow dark road. At this time, he was thankful for converting the Bronco to electric. The quiet purr of the engine allowed him to get closer than he would have been able to with the rumble of a gas-powered engine.

At a hundred yards, he discerned a break in the woods he guessed was the drop site. He threw the shifter into park and killed the engine. Once he got out, he attached his knife to his belt, checked his knuckledusters were secure in his back pockets, and then slung the MP5 over his shoulder. Quietly he closed the door. He went left and entered the cover of the woods. With the stock of the machine gun secured to his shoulder, he crept toward the clearing. His determination renewed. The steady flow of adrenaline pumping through his nervous system masked the pain in his ribs and face.

A light flared in his night vision goggles as he came within twenty yards. Crouching behind a tree, he surveyed the situation. Clayton's truck sat in another clearing similar to the first one Wyler discovered, but with less space. The three men got out and met at the trailer, each holding flashlights. Wyler edged closer, to ten yards. They spoke loud enough for him to hear.

"So, what the fuck are we supposed to do with these dogs?" guy one said as he opened the trailer door.

"The boss said we tie the dogs to this ATV thing and drive it across to the other side," guy two said, wheeling out the driverless ATV.

Guy one picked up the beefy controller to the vehicle. "You know how to drive it?"

"How fucking hard can it be?" guy two said, snatching the controller from his hands. "I'm going to work on getting it set up over here. You two start getting the dogs out."

"Aren't we supposed to let the Bama Boys know we're here?" guy three said.

"That's right," guy two said, returning to the truck's cabin. He returned with a walkie-talkie. "Boss said to use this when we got here. Channel three, he said to use."

Guy three fiddled with the walkie-talkie. Once he had it on and tuned to the right channel, he depressed the button and said, "Hello, is anybody there?" He lowered the device and chuckled. "I feel like I'm in fucking elementary school. These fucking bumpkins."

The three men laughed.

"I hate dealing with these guys," guy one said. "Backwoods mother fuckers. They're probably all fucking each other."

The comment drew more laughter. Then the walkie-talkie crackled, and a voice came through. "Who's this?"

"It's jolly ol' saint Nick," guy three said into the walkie-talkie with a grin. "Who the fuck you think it is?"

A pause, then the voice said, "You got the dogs or what?"

"Yeah, we got them."

"Start sending them then."

"Roger," guy three said. They all laughed again.

"All right, let's get this shit over with," guy two said and headed to the front of the truck with the ATV and controller. The other two guys strolled into the trailer.

"Fucking reeks in here," guy one said.

Once they disappeared inside, Wyler saw his opportunity to strike while they were separated. He dashed through the woods until he was in line with the middle of the truck and trailer so the men inside couldn't see him, and the guy working the ATV faced the other direction. Wyler sprinted from his hiding spot to the side of the truck. He crouched and maneuvered to the front wheel. If possible, he wanted to subdue the men without firing a shot. He swiveled the gun to his back and slipped a knuckleduster onto his right hand. Carefully, he peeked around the edge of the truck. Guy two stood at the rear of the ATV, focused on the controller. Wyler wished Blackjack was with him. The situation he found himself in highlighted how much he relied on his partnership with the dog. *If Blackjack didn't make it*...he stopped himself from finishing the thought. If he was going to make a move, it was now or never.

He stood and took five long strides toward guy two. His body passing in front of the truck's headlights caught guy two's attention right as Wyler got to him. Wyler swung hard, but guy two had a quick reaction time, and the blow glanced off his jaw with nowhere near the force Wyler had hoped for. The man stumbled, caught off guard by the sudden attack. Wyler threw another punch that was blocked by guy two's forearm. Then he flung the controller at Wyler. Wyler dodged the retaliation strike and lashed out with a left-handed jab striking guy two in the face. He absorbed the punch better than Wyler wanted. As Wyler threw a right-handed hook, guy two dove forward, slamming into Wyler and driving them to the ground. The man's weight compressed on Wyler's bruised ribs.

"Hey, Rocco," came the voice of guy one. "What the fuck's going on over there?"

Things were already not going according to plan for Wyler. He needed this guy down and out quickly, not the drawn-out fight it was turning into. As Wyler shook off the spreading burn through his ribs, guy two, Rocco, enclosed his strong hands around Wyler's throat and squeezed. The sudden absence of air in Wyler's lungs triggered a cacophony of alarm bells in his brain. The fingers dug into the flesh of his neck. Blackness crept in at the edges of his vision. *Do something,* his body screamed. *This isn't how your story ends. Fight.*

Wyler's hand searched the ground and got to his waist. A few more seconds and he would black out, and that would be the end. Then his fingers found the handle of his knife. He ripped it from the sheath and jammed it into Rocco's side.

"Gah," Rocco shouted. "You mother fucker."

Wyler twisted and then extracted the knife, repeating the action five more times until the hands released their death grip on his throat. As Rocco leaned back, grabbing his side, Wyler quickly shifted the knife handle to a handshake grip. Then he drove the blade into the soft flesh below Rocco's chin, sinking it into the handle. Rocco's body shuddered and pitched to the side. Wyler coughed violently, gasping for air. As Rocco's dead body slid off him, guys one and three came into view, each holding two dogs attached to short ropes. Their mouths dropped open in shock. It took them a full five seconds to comprehend what was happening. When they did, guy three released the ropes of his dogs and fumbled for the walkie-talkie. He pressed the button and shouted. "We're under attack. Send everyone you've got. Did you hear me? We've..."

Wyler fired a three-round burst into the guy's chest, cutting off further communication. The noise from the gun jarred guy one out of his stunned trance. He dropped his ropes and went for what Wyler guessed was a gun at his back.

"Don't," Wyler rasped as he swung the barrel of the MP5 level with the guy's stomach. "Don't," Wyler repeated as the guy continued the motion. When the outline of a pistol took shape, Wyler released another burst from the machine gun. Three bullets hit the guy, starting at his stomach and ending at his neck. A gurgling grunt escaped his mouth before crumpling to the grass.

With the three men dead, Wyler dropped his head to the ground, staring into the brightening early morning sky as he caught his breath. He massaged his sore neck before forcing himself to his feet. The clock still ticked in his mind. *How fast would the people on the other side of the clearing take to react to the walkie-talkie message?* Wyler assumed they heard the gunfire. *Would they chance coming across to investigate and get their drugs?* He had to move under the assumption they would.

Staggering to Rocco, Wyler placed his boot on the man's chest. Then he reached down and yanked the knife out of Rocco's head. After wiping the blood off the blade on the dead man's chest, Wyler slipped the knife into its sheath. He did a quick pat down of Rocco and removed a Glock. Repeating the process with the other dead men produced two more of the same guns. Wyler holstered one of the guns at his hip, popped the mags from the others, and stuffed them in his pockets. A movement to his right caused Wyler to spin and swing the MP5 to his shoulder, ready to cut down anyone he saw. As he saw the source of the movement, he stopped. Two of the greyhounds slunk along the treeline. Wyler lowered the gun and approached them slowly.

"It's alright," Wyler said to them. "I know you've had a tough go of things. I'm here to help."

He held out his hand for them to sniff. They backed away, exhibiting the signs of dogs exposed to terrible living conditions. Sensing they might run, he got low, and made himself as unthreatening as possible. Speaking quietly, he inched towards the dangling leashes. Avoiding eye contact, Wyler scooped up the ropes.

"There we go. I won't hurt you."

He led them to the trailer, looking for the other two dogs as he did, but they never materialized. Wyler walked the greyhounds inside and secured them in their cages. When he got outside, he slammed the trailer door closed behind him. Then he went to where the trailer was hitched to Clayton's truck. It took him under five minutes to detach and raise the coupler. He hustled to the driver's side and hopped in the truck. The keys were in the ignition. He fired up the engine and drove the truck into the space leading to the connecting path to the gang on the other side. The width of the truck blocked any large vehicles from entering.

Wyler jumped out and then ran down the dirt road from where he initially followed Rocco into the clearing. Three minutes later, he arrived at the Bronco. *Taking too long. Move faster.* Exhausted, he got in, turned it on, and then raced to the trailer. He had enough room to maneuver and align the rear of the Bronco with the coupler. Using his mirrors, he stopped when he thought he was close enough to make the connection. He leaped out to check. *Move. Make it quick. Time is not on your side.* A few more inches and he was there.

Sid stared into the blackness. The frantic message and gunshots got his blood pumping and running hot. *What the fuck was going on? Who was out there? Who would be dumb enough to make a play against them?* Then a smile slowly spread on Sid's face. A smile laced with hate and revenge. A smile of knowing. *It's him. It's got to be him. That prick and the mutt.*

"Get the dirt bikes," Sid said with sadistic excitement as he imagined the violent things he was about to do. "Strap up."

"You want to go over there?" one of his cousins said.

"Fuck yeah. Someone's trying to rip us off. You want to let them?"

"What about the state lines?"

"Fuck the state lines."

"What if it's the cops?"

"Get the fucking bikes." Sid shouted.

No one else protested. Men scattered, running to get the smaller vehicles. Sid flung the door open to his truck. He snatched an assault rifle mounted to the rear window. From the glove box, he rooted out two thirty round magazines.

"Hurry up." Sid shouted to the men. "Hurry the fuck up."

He slammed a magazine into the rifle and charged the bolt. The men led three bikes over. Sid shoved aside one of them with an animalistic snarl. His blood was on fire. His vision tunneled. *Gonna kill those mother fuckers.*

"If any of you pussies bail, I'll put a bullet in you too," Sid said, mounting the dirt bike. "Let's fucking go."

He slung his rifle over his back. After kicking the engine to life, Sid tilted his head toward the sky and howled.

Wyler heard a noise in the distance. He paused to listen. His ears strained to determine what it was. Then he recognized the sound of small engines. Dirt bikes.

"Shit," he said, knowing people were coming. The sound was faint. He guessed he had less than three minutes before whoever it was arrived. *Need more time. Need a distraction. Something to deter an all-out attack.* He grabbed the MP5 and glanced around the space for the spark of an idea. He ducked inside Clayton's truck, searching for anything useful. A lighter sat in a tray beneath the dash. Wyler glanced out the windshield and spotted three pinheads of light two hundred yards off. His window of opportunity was closing.

He turned on the truck's engine and then snatched the lighter, along with a bandana, from the tray. Then he hustled to the truck's rear and opened the latch to the gas tank. With his index finger, he stuffed the bandana into the hole as far as it would go. Wyler kept the driver-side door open and shouldered the MP5. He rested the barrel in the groove between the frame. The lights were more prominent now, maybe only fifty yards away. Wyler took a deep breath in. He brought the sights onto the headlight of the dirt bike farthest to the left. As he exhaled, Wyler squeezed the trigger. A three-round burst. The headlight wobbled, then vanished. Wyler shifted the sights quickly to the target farthest to the right. Another burst of three rounds. The light swerved but remained on. Then he focused on the center light and fired until the magazine emptied.

Without waiting to see the results, Wyler darted to the bandana at the gas tank and lit it. He sprinted back to the truck cabin, where he jammed the MP5 into the base of the driver's seat so the stock depressed the gas pedal. Reaching to the right of the steering wheel, he wrenched the shifter into drive. The sudden jolt launched Wyler clear of the truck. Laying on the ground, he watched as the vehicle sped down the narrow path. Shouts followed and the whine of the dirt bikes braking hard. The truck hit a bump and lurched to the left. It smashed into a tree, but the impact didn't kill the engine. The wheels continued spinning, kicking up dirt.

Wyler pushed to his feet and ran to the Bronco. Leaving the door open, he tapped the pedal, reversing the remaining few inches to link with the trailer. He hurried to the connection points and cranked the handle on the hitch, lowering the coupler onto the ball attached to the Bronco. His hands flew over the connecting chains and plugged in the tail light wires. As he was about to get into the SUV, a shot rang out. A searing hot pain sliced through Wyler's left arm. He fell into the side of the Bronco and dropped to the ground. More bullets chewed up the earth around him. Wyler crawled under the vehicle to the other side. Staying low, he dabbed at his arm. *No entry wound, just a graze.*

"Come on out, you rat bastard," a voice shouted. "I'm going to rip your fucking guts out through your ass hole."

Wyler crouched, drawing the Glock. He peeked around the edge. The headlights from the Bronco allowed him to see some-one at the clearing exit. *Sid.* A bullet pinged off of the hood, and Wyler ducked back. He needed to draw the fire away from the vehicle. If a bullet tore through something vital in the engine, he'd be stranded.

"Where are you, you little pussy? I know it's you." Sid shouted. "Think you can fuck with us and get away with it?"

More shots ripped up the grass around him. Wyler was pretty sure Sid had some type of assault rifle. If Wyler made a dash for it, he could get cut down. A bullet knocked out a headlight. He needed to move before it was too late. Then the flame found its way into the gas tank of Clayton's truck. A second later, it ignited. A deafening blast spread through the air as the truck erupted.

Wyler seized the moment, and dove from cover, rolling into the open. He stopped on his stomach with the Glock forward. His sights landed on Sid, who was crouched, turning toward the inferno behind him. Wyler squeezed off a rapid-fire onslaught of bullets. The Glock barked like a hound from hell. On the third shot, a round connected with Sid near his stomach. With his aim zeroed in, Wyler fired until the slide locked open from the spent magazine. He ejected the magazine deftly, rammed home a fresh one, and kept the gun leveled on Sid's crumpled form. When he was sure Sid was down for the count, Wyler staggered to his feet.

Keeping the gun sweeping over the area of the burning truck, he sidestepped in front of the Bronco and then backpedaled until he reached the driver's side door. In the trailer, the dogs barked in distress from all the noise. Wyler held his breath as he got in the driver seat, praying none of the bullets damaged anything. As he scanned the console, everything still seemed in working order. Wyler released his breath. He shifted into reverse and navigated the Bronco through the narrow path. His fingers dug into the wheel from his coiled nerves. He didn't want to go too slow and give Sid's people time to catch up with him, but he also didn't want to push the speed to where he couldn't control it. One wrong turn and the trailer could slam into a tree, creating a host of new problems. His eyes darted back and forth to each side mirror, easing the steering wheel to compensate for the subtle turns in the terrain.

He drove only two hundred yards, yet it felt like it took five hours. Sweat dripped, burning into his eyes, but he didn't dare take his hands from the wheel. Then the ground smoothed out, and he was free of the woods. Back on the main road, Wyler kept reversing until he could straighten out. Then he took one final glance down the path, ensuring no one was following him. Satisfied he was clear, Wyler shifted into drive and sped off with the trailer full of greyhounds.

Chapter 24

Wyler drove for an hour into the early morning, putting as much distance behind him as he could. When he felt safe, he pulled off at a rest area. After Wyler plugged in the Bronco, he grabbed his medical kit and inspected the wound on his arm. The bullet had created a decent gash. A few inches to the right, the bullet would have found solid mass. Wyler poured antiseptic over the wound, then dabbed it dry. He realistically would need stitches, but for the time being, a healthy dose of liquid bandage would have to do. When he finished with his arm, Wyler poured water over his face, dried it, and then applied a thin layer of petroleum to the cuts on his cheek. He downed three painkillers last.

Wyler rummaged around until he found the burner phone. He called Arlo while he paced outside the Bronco.

Arlo answered on the third ring. "Declan?" Arlo paused, and then he said with genuine concern, "Are you alright?"

"Things went a little left, but I'm ok," Wyler said. "I've got them.

I've got the dogs. How are you doing with the handoff team?"

"They're all set. Tell me where you need them."

"Where are they coming from?" Wyler said, pulling up a map on his personal phone.

"Atlanta."

Wyler zoomed in on the map. "Have them meet me outside of Montgomery. Hold on a second, and I'll read you the coordinates."

"Ok."

Wyler dropped a pin on the map, then read the coordinates to Arlo, directing the handoff team to a remote area.

"Alright, I've got it. I'll get them moving now," Arlo said.

After a moment of dead air, Arlo said, "Is there something else?"

"It's Blackjack," Wyler said. "He...he took two rounds to the leg. I brought him to the hospital that worked on the original greyhound. The guy working on him, I think we can trust him, but it might not be a bad idea to send them a sizable donation to keep it that way."

Arlo didn't immediately respond. Then he said, "Is Blackjack..."

"I don't know. He's my next stop after I drop off the greyhounds."

"I'm sorry, Declan." Arlo paused. "I'll take care of any of the expenses associated with it. And I'll see to the donation. It's a smart idea."

"Alright. I should hit the road."

"We'll talk soon."

After ending the call, Wyler made himself an instant brew coffee with his camp stove. When the Bronco finished charging, he climbed in and set off.

An hour later, Wyler parked on a desolate road overlooking the Tallapoosa River. He got out and went to the trailer, detached the chains, and raised the coupler from the Bronco. Then he threw open the trailer doors, allowing fresh air into the putrid-smelling enclosure. The dogs stirred at his presence. He walked in and spoke to them in a reassuring voice.

"You're safe now. It's almost over."

He checked the cages to assess the state of each greyhound. Most of them were in rough shape. At least three of them, he estimated, wouldn't make the final leg of the journey. For those who made it, though, those who survived, they'd live out their remaining years in peace. They had earned it. Knowing that made everything he'd gone through the last few days worth it. Saving the greyhounds gave him some small sense of redemption for the dogs who died while under his care over the years. It gave him a glimmer of hope the pieces of himself he thought lost forever could be restored.

He went outside then and waited for Arlo's guys. Forty-five minutes later, a twenty-six-foot U-Haul truck pulled alongside Wyler.

"Heard you needed a pickup," the driver said in a deep baritone voice.

Wyler grinned at seeing the familiar face. Tate Kingston opened the door and jumped down. He was tall and fit with a broad smile, a precisely lined head of short black hair, and a neatly trimmed beard. He wore dark blue jeans, Nikes, and a gray t-shirt with the logo of his gym printed on the front. Wyler and Arlo knew Tate from their days in the Marines. Tate served as a field medic, and when he left the service, he worked as an EMT for years. The last Wyler had heard from him, he was opening his own mixed martial arts gym.

"So, Arlo got you wrangled into this too, huh?" Wyler said as the old friends shook hands.

Tate shrugged and smiled. "What can I say? The man speaks the universal language of cash money. Plus, I have a hard time saying no to friends. So here I am."

A woman came around the front of the truck.

"Hello, Imani," Wyler said to Tate's wife. Wyler always thought she was a dead ringer for Angela Bassett in her prime. Tall, elegant, and beautiful. She met Tate while on the job, working as an EMT in Philadelphia before moving on to the veterinary profession.

"Declan," she said. After giving him a hug, she stepped back, studying him. "I mean this in the nicest way possible, but you look like shit."

Wyler shrugged. "Being rough around the edges is part of my charm."

"Well, then, you must be the most charming man in the world."

"You need me to patch you up?" Tate said, pointing at Wyler's arm.

"After we get the dogs out of here. How much did Arlo tell you?"

"Said some dogs needed to be brought to his sanctuary. Told us they were banged up and would need medical attention. Something about them being drug mules. That about sum it up?"

"Pretty much."

"What kind of dogs are we dealing with?" Tate said.

"Greyhounds. Close to thirty of them. I'm not sure how many of them have drugs inside them."

"What kind of drugs?" Imani asked.

"Fentanyl."

Tate and Imani nodded.

"Well," Tate said. "Show us what we're dealing with."

They reached the trailer. Tate and Imani walked in, covering their mouths and noses with their shirts. When they came out, Tate said, "It's not pretty."

"You take care of the bastards that did it, at least?" Imani asked.

"As many as I could."

"Good," she said. "Let's get them unloaded."

The three of them coaxed the dogs from their cages and walked or carried those who couldn't to the U-Haul. Tate slid open the large rear door. Instead of the cold empty container Wyler expected to see, the inside looked like a first-class hospital on wheels. Glass enclosures stacked three high lined the two side walls stretching from the door to three-thirds of the length of the storage area. Plush dog beds covered the floor of each. Warm, soft light flooded the interior. At the back wall, a medical table was flanked by cabinets containing every medical supply known to man.

"What the hell is this?" Wyler said.

"That's what we said when we picked the truck up," Tate said. "Arlo, man. That guy thinks of everything. This isn't something you whip together in a few hours. He must have had this ready for years."

"He doesn't do anything half-assed. I'll give him that."

"Nope."

Wyler passed his dogs to Tate and then hoisted himself into the U-Haul. He opened the door of the lowest level of enclosures. Tate then handed the first dog to Wyler. He felt the bones of the emaciated body as he eased it into the holding area. After twenty minutes, they transferred all of the greyhounds to the U-Haul.

"Should we stitch that arm of yours now?" Tate asked Wyler.

"Might as well."

The three of them climbed into the traveling hospital. Tate inspected the gash on Wyler's arm. "I think you'll live."

"Make it quick."

Tate grabbed a couple of supplies from the cabinets, and then the two of them moved out of the way allowing Imani to work on the dogs.

"So what was all this about?" Tate asked as he threaded a needle.

Wyler recapped the events of the last few days, starting with his initial meeting with Arlo. Then he took Tate through how he tracked down the dogs, his encounter with Sid, and what they were doing at the Klempt farm. Then he told him about the shootout at Clayton's and how he ultimately got the dogs.

"Sounds like you brought hell to these people," Tate said as he finished the suture.

Wyler shrugged. "I tried to, anyway." He got up and inspected his arm. "Thanks."

"Glad I could help," Tate said as he returned the supplies to the cabinet. "How you been otherwise? You still knocking around AC?"

"Yeah, I'm still there. What's new with you two? Any baby Kingstons on the way?"

Imani laughed. "Our professions are our children."

"She's not wrong about that," Tate said. "You make an honest woman out of Enola yet?"

"Tate," Imani said over her shoulder. Her eyes like daggers.

"What?"

Wyler rubbed the back of his neck. "We're not together anymore."

"I told you that," Imani said. "You don't listen for shit."

Tate put one hand on his chest, frowning. "My bad, man. I didn't...I...ah, hell."

"Forget it," Wyler said. He cleared his throat in the awkward silence that followed. "Well, I should be on my way." Wyler moved to Imani then and put his hand on her shoulder. "Thanks for doing this."

"You did good work here, Declan," Imani said, giving him a farewell hug. "We'll take it from here." She nodded at Tate. "And don't mind that idiot. I'll ream him out for bringing her up once we get moving."

Wyler grinned.

"Will we see you at the sanctuary?" she asked.

"I'll be by in a few days."

"Well, take care of yourself in the meantime," she said and then looked at Tate. "And you, drive slow."

"It'll be as if we're floating on clouds," Tate answered with a grin.

She rolled her eyes before returning to her work. Wyler hopped out of the U-Haul, and Tate followed him, closing the door behind them.

"Where are you off to now?" Tate asked as they walked towards their respective vehicles.

"I've got to get Blackjack, and then I'm done."

"Listen, I'm sorry for bringing her up. I think we're overdue for a beer anyway. Tab's on me next time to make it up to you."

"I'll hold you to it."

They shook hands and embraced each other with a pat on the back.

"Take it easy, brother," Tate said.

"You too."

Wyler climbed stiffly back into the Bronco and started it. He had roughly a two-hour drive ahead of him. He hoped it was enough time to prepare for the news that awaited him about Blackjack.

Wyler arrived at the animal hospital at eight in the morning. He took a deep breath and called Hudson.

"Hello," Hudson answered.

"It's me. I'm here."

"Alright. Hold on. I'm inside. I'll be out in a minute to let you in."

The call ended, and Wyler exited the Bronco and went to the door. He felt lightheaded as his anxiety flared about what Hudson would tell him. A minute later, the door opened. Hudson waved him in. Wyler studied the man's face for any signs of bad news. A mask of exhaustion covered his face, but he made eye contact, which Wyler found encouraging.

"Well?" Wyler said.

Hudson put his hand on Wyler's shoulder. Wyler felt as though the Grim Reaper had just touched him.

"He's alive."

The tension in Wyler's body relaxed. He exhaled and nodded in gratitude.

"Come on, I'll take you to him."

Hudson led Wyler down a hallway and entered a recovery room with three crates. Blackjack rested on his side in the middle one. His leg was shaved down to the skin, and bandages covered the wounds. When he saw Wyler, his head raised, and his tail flapped with excitement against the cushion he laid on. Fighting back the urge to cry, Wyler crouched and said to him, "You ready to go home, boy?"

Wyler opened the crate and petted Blackjack's head as he attempted to stand.

"It's alright. Don't get up," Wyler said.

Hudson said, "He'll be drowsy for a while from the sedatives and painkillers. And the hair will grow back before you know it. Thankfully, the bullet in the meat of his leg didn't go deep, and it didn't fragment. I was able to extract it with minimal effort. I took an x-ray and didn't see damage done to any bones. Both wounds got stitches. I also gave him an antibiotic to play it safe. He'll need a lot of rest, and he'll be sore for a while, but overall, he should pull through. He's tough. I can tell he's got a warrior spirit."

Wyler struggled for words. He cleared his throat, gathering his composure, and said, "Thank you. Seriously. Thank you."

"It's my job. No thanks needed."

"And did anyone ask about him?" Wyler said as he stood to face Hudson.

"I wrote him up as a stray I found. We're all here because we love animals, especially dogs. And you seem to be one of the good ones fighting for them, so we've got you. If anything comes back on you, it won't be from us."

Wyler nodded. He then reached into his pocket and took out his wallet. From it, he pulled a card with a unique number associated with Arlo. Wyler handed it to Hudson.

"I owe you one. If you ever need anything—and I mean anything—call that number, and you'll get it."

Hudson stared at the card and then slipped it into a pocket of his scrubs.

"Ok," he said. Then he went to a counter and tossed a few bottles of pills into a brown bag. "These are the rest of the antibiotics and his painkillers. Instructions are on the bottles."

Wyler took the bag and shook Hudson's hand. "Thanks again."

Wyler bent down and gently scooped Blackjack up. The gash on his arm throbbed under the dead weight of the dog, but he didn't care. He would've gladly given his whole arm if it meant Blackjack would live. As Wyler rose, Blackjack bent his head and licked Wyler on the side of the face. Smiling, Wyler said, "Don't go getting sentimental on me now."

Hudson led them down the hallway and held open the back door. Halfway to the Bronco, Wyler stopped and said, "Hey, and if you see a donation come through to the hospital, know that's from my people and me."

"Ok," Hudson said. "That's not necessary, but ok."

At the Bronco, Hudson opened the rear gate, and Wyler eased Blackjack down and covered him with a blanket. With his friend safe and secure, Wyler turned to Hudson.

"Thanks again. I won't forget this."

Hudson nodded.

Wyler reversed and then drove out of the lot toward the last stop of his journey.

Chapter 25

Wyler split up the nearly twelve-hour drive to Virginia over two days. The first night they stopped over the South Carolina border in a scenic area overlooking Lake Hartwell. Using a folded blanket, Wyler fashioned a sling to loop under Blackjack to keep him upright while he relieved himself. Wyler didn't go far from the dog the entire night, worrying over him like a mother hen. The painkillers allowed Blackjack to sleep, which Wyler was thankful for.

In the morning, they set off early and arrived at the Blackstone dog sanctuary in rural Virginia. The sanctuary occupied nearly fifty acres of land. Wyler drove under the arch serving as the entrance to the sprawling landscape. An old frontier-style fence surrounded the entirety of the property. State-of-the-art security cameras and sensors protected the land. Much of the technology came from the advances implemented at the southern border. Regarding security, Arlo never scrimped on shelling out the big bucks. The paved road wound through a dense forest until it opened to the main patch of cleared land housing the facilities.

Wyler stopped the Bronco at a sturdier gate enclosing twenty acres of wilderness. He pressed the button beneath an intercom and camera. No one spoke to him. The gate simply opened as he was a known face at the sanctuary. The road led to a massive house that Arlo and the people who ran the facilities on a day-to-day basis lived in. Like everything Arlo did, the house was designed with meticulous precision. The architects who built it employed every piece of modern knowledge about sustainability. Power came from solar roofing and a dedicated wind farm located to the west of the property, which created enough energy to sustain every building on the premises. Geothermal devices heated and cooled each structure. And a large satellite dish kept them connected to the outside world.

Behind the house were two other large, sustainably constructed, and thought-through buildings. One was a dedicated greenhouse that produced enough food year-round to feed the entire staff and the dogs that came into the sanctuary. The other served as a hospital, research lab, training facility, and housing quarters for the dogs. Beyond that, another two-acre plot of land was fenced in where the dogs roamed free. As a whole, the Blackstone dog sanctuary was one part Silicon Valley and one part ecological preserve.

Wyler drove around the house and parked between the hospital and the greenhouse, where he had a view of the dog field. He recognized the figure inside watching the dogs. Wyler leaned over the seat. Blackjack popped an eye open.

"I'll be right back," Wyler said to him. Blackjack didn't object and resumed his slumber. Before heading to the field, Wyler opened the back window so Blackjack had some fresh air.

Wyler pushed through the gate and stopped when he was side by side with Arlo.

"Still in one piece, I see," Arlo said, keeping his attention on the dogs.

"Mostly."

A dog approached Wyler. It was a greyhound. The animal sniffed his leg, then rubbed against him as if he knew what Wyler had done for him. Wyler petted the dog for a few seconds before it leaped off and chased after another dog running past.

"That's one of yours," Arlo said.

To see a dog on the road to a better life as a direct result of his actions put a humble smile on Wyler's face. It touched a deep part of his heart that he thought was scarred over. "I'm surprised to see any of them running around."

"These couple out here are the exception. Two days of real food, water, and affection do wonders. They've got a stretch of recovery ahead of them still, but it's an encouraging sign."

"What's the initial assessment?"

"We logged twenty-eight greyhounds in total. Ten of them had packets of drugs in their lower intestines. We managed to successfully remove the packets from all but two. A seam had opened in their containers, exposing them to the fentanyl beyond the point of saving, unfortunately. We had to put down one more of them that was too far gone. Of the twenty-five left, the team is optimistic. They're confident at least twenty of them will reach a full recovery and go on to live healthy lives. The other five have some extra needs, but the team thinks with time they'll recover too."

"I lost two of them at the end. They got away from me. Things were chaotic."

"You don't need to justify anything to me."

"And the ten others. I couldn't save them. I had to watch them die."

Arlo nodded in understanding. "If it wasn't for you, twenty-five more dogs would have met the same fate."

"Just look on the bright side, is that it?"

"Something like that."

"It's hard to share in the sentiment when you're exposed to the worst in people."

Arlo said nothing. After a moment, he extracted an envelope from his pocket. He handed it to Wyler.

"What's this?"

"The rest of your payment for the job. Plus a bonus for going above and beyond."

Wyler peeled back part of the envelope and glanced at the contents. From his estimate, the bundles of cash were at least twenty grand over the remaining amount Arlo owed him.

"That's rather generous," Wyler said.

"You earned it." Arlo looked at Wyler then. "Is there anything else I need to be aware of as to what you left behind? Is there a body count?"

Wyler nodded.

"How many?" Arlo asked without judgment.

Wyler went through the last few days in his head. *Nine. Nine people dead.* He let the number sink in. *Jesus, was it that many? They butchered innocent dogs, though. The drugs they moved would've destroyed countless lives. The right decision was made. The world will be better without them.* He hung on to the justification as he spoke. "Nine confirmed, and maybe two unconfirmed. At least three or four more will have a hospital bill to pay off."

Arlo nodded solemnly. "Are there any links to you that need breaking?"

"I don't think so. Whoever is left wouldn't be eager to talk to the cops on a good day, if you know what I mean. Couldn't hurt though to have Mack keep an eye on any chatter for the next few months."

"And our contact at the animal hospital?"

"He's solid."

"Does he have to worry about his safety?"

Wyler paused, thinking. "There's not much tying him to what happened. He can't give anyone much useful information. Not that I can see anyway. If you've got a place for him though, it wouldn't hurt to see if he's open to relocating."

"Alright. I'll look into it."

Another dog, a mutt, part lab and some sort of collie, ran up to Arlo with a ball in its mouth. Arlo wrangled the ball free and chucked it, which the dog happily chased down.

"You're welcome to stay here a while if you'd like," Arlo said. "Stick around, and see the good you've done. Help train some of these dogs. Let Blackjack heal. What do you think?"

Wyler shrugged. "It's tempting, but I'm ready to lie in my own bed for a while."

"Well, you have a standing invitation."

"I'll keep that in mind."

Arlo's phone buzzed then. He checked the screen.

"I need to take this."

"I'll see myself out."

They shook hands.

"Thank you, Declan," Arlo said with a straight face of sincerity. "You did a good thing here."

Wyler nodded and then turned, leaving Arlo to his call. As he approached the Bronco, a pair of shapely legs dangled from the open back gate. Wyler's heart quickened.

"What have you done to this poor baby?" Enola Harjo said to Wyler as he stopped a few feet from her. Blackjack's head rested in her lap, and she gently stroked his fur. A look of blissful contentment covered the dog's face. Wyler gazed at the former love of his life. She wore her silky black hair in a loose ponytail draped across her shoulder. A pair of skinny jeans hugged her hips, and a patterned blouse flowed in the light breeze. The sight of her stirred up emotions he'd mostly suppressed until this very moment.

"I swear we don't go looking for trouble," Wyler said.

"But it always manages to find you, doesn't it?" she said with more sarcasm than anger. Enola looked at Wyler then. Her warm brown eyes on him again after their time apart forced him to focus on the ground. He wasn't prepared for her beauty.

"If you keep pampering him like that, he'll be lost to me forever," Wyler said.

"Maybe," she said with a grin as she returned her attention to Blackjack. "You know there are easier ways to get my attention, don't you?"

Wyler shrugged, "I wasn't sure you'd answer a simple phone call."

She forced a smile and changed the subject. "How has Blackjack been doing with his sign language and vocabulary?"

"Makes progress every day."

"That's because you're brilliant, aren't you?" she said in a matter-of-fact tone to Blackjack. She and Wyler made a pact to never speak to the dog in a baby voice, and despite their time apart, they'd both stuck to the promise. She continued to run her slender fingers through Blackjack's fur. "Should I bother asking where you found these greyhounds?"

"Only if you want to make me a liar."

Enola frowned. "It's funny. Arlo had a similar response." She turned her head slightly to glance at him. "Are you staying a while?"

He didn't want to read too much into the question or the look on her face, but a part of him felt she wouldn't be upset if he said yes.

"No. I've got to get him home. Get him back on his feet," Wyler said. "Besides, I wouldn't want to be a distraction." He should've left the last part out, but seeing her brought back some painful memories. She ended things to focus on her work. And he left as a result. Her eyes filled with hurt from his not-so-subtle dig.

"Declan..." she said, but was cut off by a coworker calling to her from the lab facility entrance. Enola waved to the coworker, acknowledging them.

"Well, I should let you get back to it," Wyler said.

Enola pet Blackjack a final time on the head before easing out from under him. Blackjack groaned in protest as she hopped off the bed door. She stood a foot from Wyler. The familiar fragrance of her drifted into Wyler's nose. He wanted to grab her, pull her tight against his chest and never let go. He wanted to kiss her and tell her his world was dark without her brightness. His heart skipped a beat as she leaned in close and kissed him softly on the cheek.

"If anything else happens to that dog again," she said. "There'll be no place on this earth you can hide from me."

Wyler smiled. "Noted."

Her eyes lingered on him a moment longer, then she turned and walked away. Wyler and Blackjack watched her until she disappeared into the building. Blackjack sighed as he sank into his bed.

"I know," Wyler said, scratching Blackjack behind the ear, feeling like he could sleep for a week. "I miss her too."

END OF BOOK 1

FOLLOW ME ON:

INSTAGRAM
MATTDURANDUSA

FACEBOOK
MATTDURANDWRITES

FOR MORE VISIT
WWW.MATTDURAND.WORK